William C. Young is an avid reader of sci-fi and alternative history. He finally got enough courage to put his love of this into words, creating a space saga, and introducing everyone to Parvon Zin's danger-filled universe. He now lives in Perth, Australia, enjoying the Aussie lifestyle and sun.

To you, my reader. Thank you.

May my stories take you on the adventure of a lifetime.

William C. Young

PARVON ZIN
KOBAN HUNTER BOOK 5:
HUNTER'S MOON

AUSTIN MACAULEY PUBLISHERS
LONDON * CAMBRIDGE * NEW YORK * SHARJAH

Copyright © William C. Young 2025

The right of William C. Young to be identified as author of this work has been asserted by the author in accordance with sections 77 and 78 of the Copyright, Designs and Patents Act 1988.

All rights reserved. No part of this publication may be reproduced, stored in a retrieval system, or transmitted in any form or by any means, electronic, mechanical, photocopying, recording, or otherwise, without the prior permission of the publishers.

Any person who commits any unauthorised act in relation to this publication may be liable to criminal prosecution and civil claims for damages.

This is a work of fiction. Names, characters, businesses, places, events, locales, and incidents are either the products of the author's imagination or used in a fictitious manner. Any resemblance to actual persons, living or dead, or actual events is purely coincidental.

A CIP catalogue record for this title is available from the British Library.

ISBN 9781035891146 (Paperback)
ISBN 9781035891153 (ePub e-book)

www.austinmacauley.com

First Published 2025
Austin Macauley Publishers Ltd®
1 Canada Square
Canary Wharf
London
E14 5AA

Thanks to Austin Macauley Publishers for their continued belief and support.

# Table of Contents

| | |
|---|---:|
| **Glossary** | 13 |
| **Gimaldreys Station Leeken's Gun Emporium** | 18 |
| **Thera Three Present Day** | 23 |
| **Anibuna Ninety-Nines, Thera Three Safari Experience** | 24 |
| **Lunderon** | 27 |
| **Thera Three, Anibuna's Mansion Madera** | 30 |
| **Thera Three Spaceport Azores Islands** | 31 |
| **Andrend Maxus Brood Commander Fedoon Belatan Peacekeeping Force** | 44 |
| **North Korea** | 49 |
| **Eden Base Control Room** | 50 |
| **Tokyo Japan** | 51 |
| **Edinburgh Scotland** | 53 |
| **Mosquerio Island Para Brazil** | 57 |
| **Ryongsong District Kim Jong-un's Central Luxury Mansion** | 61 |

| | |
|---|---|
| **Kirkland AFB** | 63 |
| **Thera Three Spaceport Ponta Delgada, Azores Islands** | 68 |
| **Ryongsong District, Central Luxury Mansion North Korea** | 72 |
| **Florida, USA** | 75 |
| **Eden Base Control Room** | 79 |
| **Ramadi Iraq 2004** | 80 |
| **Games Sports Channel Present Day** | 85 |
| **Leeken's Gunsmithing Workshop** | 95 |
| **Inipan of the Anisol** | 97 |
| **Anibuna's Office, Madera** | 108 |
| **Lunderon's Transport Shuttle** | 109 |
| **Eden Base, Joadin's Office** | 110 |
| **San Francisco, USA** | 115 |
| **Lunderon** | 120 |
| **SRC51's Temporary Base Jan Mayen Island, Arctic Circle** | 123 |
| **Porto Alegre Uruguay, South America** | 125 |
| **Lunderon** | 130 |
| **Anibuna's Mansion Madera** | 131 |
| **Lunderon** | 134 |
| **Thera Three Australian Outback** | 135 |

| | |
|---|---|
| **Eden Base Control Room** | 136 |
| **Anibuna's Mansion, Madera** | 141 |
| **Anibuna's Conquest Ship The Anun** | 143 |
| **Eden Base Security Cells** | 146 |
| **Randor SID Main Office** | 148 |
| **Eden Base** | 149 |
| **Parvon Training Ground on Randor's Second Moon Kessron 2AIA** | 150 |
| **Thera Three Games Procurement Stevedores** | 153 |
| **The Hollers Harlan County, Kentucky** | 155 |
| **Polyrend Four Second Arm of the Spiral Galaxy** | 159 |
| **Eden Base Hangar Deck** | 160 |
| **Gishma Leadership Complex, Planet Bleopan** | 164 |
| **Kentucky National Guard Building, Harlan County** | 169 |
| **Anibuna's Conquest Ship The Anun** | 172 |
| **Mars Orbit** | 176 |
| **Harlan County** | 178 |
| **Dovernn One Gishma Clan Leader** | 181 |
| **Eden Base** | 183 |

# Glossary

**ANUNNAKI.** Birdlike reptilians with a bird's head, vestigial wings and powerful body. They are slavers and lust for gold. Not a part of the Alliance of planets, their arrogance forbids it.

**BELATANS.** Squat iguana-like bipedal reptilians, bankers and lawyers, all Alliance business is done through Belatan. Very powerful beings as they hold most of the secrets of each race. Ruthless when it comes to money or law.

**BOLDONIANS.** Most humanoid-looking of the reptilians, merchants supplying the Alliance with everything sellable, gentle beings until their business is threatened; then they declare war until it is resolved; they have a vast armada of merchant ships, heavily armed merchant ships.

**ENDINEKI.** Scientists, engineers, and medical specialists. Looking like bipedal geckos. The entire planet is focused on these disciplines. Highly sought after as healers and teachers.

**HUMANS.** Non-shape shifting beings. Genetically altered by the Gishma tribe of the Anunnaki to be a slave species and to work the gold mines on Thera Three (Earth). Or as the

Anunnaki named them when they created what is now modern man. Adamu.

**KOBAN.** The only true parasitic shape shifter, snake-like; on hatching, it must subsume a host to survive and grow. The females return to their snake form when mature enough to explosively leave the planet it plundered to spawn, using a volcanic thermal vent to get it into space. Now known to be a genetic weapon created by the Gishma clan of the Anunnaki.

**POLTOX.** Alligators on legs, a very aggressive species; they hire out to any species as security guards and mercenaries; very loose ties to the Alliance. Brood groups are small units from individual clans that hire out independently, there are usually two hundred and fifty Poltox in a brood group.

**RANDORIANS.** Oldest of the reptilians, and developers of the Star Drive system, thought to be do-gooders by some. The Randorians are the main component of the Koban hunting teams.

**SILVENEXIANS.** Insectoid race with three separate species, Red, Blue, and Black, secretive, and sly; they are not trusted by the reptilians.

**THIBRANS.** Smallest of the reptilians, with a large round head atop a spindly body, barely five feet high, timid, and cowardly. They were totally subjugated by the Anistol Anunnaki aeons ago and made into their slaves. They are the Anunnaki's servants, doing whatever is required by their overlords and masters.

Anibuna is delighted with himself. He is dancing a little jig in the palatial games room of his house in Madera. His purple and red-tipped wings flare out, and his feathered head crest rises up showing a visual display of his prowess. His brag-bag has just informed him he is now in the much sought after strata of the Gishma Clan as being a 'Twosy.' He is ninety-ninth on the Gishma hierarchy leaderboard. Having just two figures after your name is a milestone very few gain, and Anibuna will not be satisfied until he is a 'Sub'. An under ten. The top ten Gishma are treated like gods.

Petral, his clan leader holds the number seven slot within the top ten Gishma leaders. He had personally given Anibuna the news of his rise in status. A great honour.

The gold flowing out of Thera Three is staggering. Petral had hinted at further advancement because of this. Joadin achieved the number one position in the science rankings. Anibuna will push for more. He just needs an angle.

Calling out to his Thibrans, he orders them to fetch him some wine and finger food. Pointing to another, he gets him to turn on the view screen and select the Games channel.

He settles into his specially made chair which has a slot for his tail in the plush cushioned back. The chair also has a vibration and heat function, incorporating a footrest and special cup holder that keeps his drinks hot or cold depending on which setting is used. He is surprised to see that the Games logo, recognisable anywhere in the galaxy, has been changed. Why would they do that?

He quickly scrolls to the Games infonet and starts to read. He is shocked to see that Kollexx has sold the Games! To Silvenex of all things! And he and the entire Yonath leadership have left for pastures new. There is even footage of Kollexx himself waving goodbye to an ecstatic crowd as he boarded a deep-space luxury transporter. Scrolling further into the news section, he reads that a dissident faction of Anunnaki has caused trouble because the new games are bloodless. Slaves or wild creatures are no longer to be involved.

Anibuna sits back in his chair. Fingers steepled under his beak, deep in thought. Then with an evil grin, which for a rigid billed Anunnaki is for the bottom of the bill to kink to one side and the tongue to slightly protrude; Anibuna by all accounts has a truly evil grin. He sends out messages to several Anunnaki he knows from different clans and puts out an interesting idea. When it comes to the Games, old rivalries are put aside.

The responses are overwhelming support of his little, interesting, money-spinning, rank-elevating idea…Anibuna will host a reborn Anunnaki-flavoured Games with more blood than they could ever possibly dream of.

He will open Thera Three as a hunting reserve without a bag limit. The rogue wild Adamu that are still scattered about the planet will be lucratively dealt with, and he will charge top credit for the hunting licences to ensure so. The galactic infrastructure for the Games is still functioning. Their media and Galactinet sites are still running. Anibuna contacts them to broach his idea. The reply is an enthusiastic one. They will cover Anibuna's enterprise as if it were the Games itself.

Doing another little jig in his room, he starts to work out various prices for landing fees, hotels, houses for the hunters to use, food, and Thibrans to use as beaters and to carry back trophies. He knows the savage creatures that were used in the arenas. He may introduce them as more exotic prey to enhance the hunt. He does his little happy dance again and calls up some people to go get reptiles for his new project.

He gets an immediate reply from a supplier that has stock that was supposed to be delivered to the Games but was cancelled at the last minute when the bleeding-hearted, scaleripped, Silvenex stopped their use in the Games. If Anibuna wants them, he can have the lot at a bargain price as they have been in cages too long as it is, and it has driven them slightly mad. Anibuna agrees at once.

The first delivery of a thousand pissed-off Conpex and a mixed bag of three hundred Janarks and Nomals will be dropped in the Middle of Australia. The hot dry climate is ideal for these reptiles. The poor Kangaroos don't know how bad the outback is about to become. Australia will be his holding area for the beasts until he uses them to seed pre-chosen hunting areas elsewhere on the planet.

Some of the Anunnaki he has contacted ask if they can bring their 'hunting dogs' with them. A lot of Anunnaki still have Silvenex slaves collared to obey. Anibuna still has his three Blues on the planet somewhere and quite a spectacle is made between rival hunters to see whose 'dog' is best. Most of these Silvenex are so beaten that they no longer have a mind of their own.

Anibuna's 'Adamu and Wildlife Safari Enterprise' is about to open its doors to the paying public.

# Gimaldreys Station
# Leeken's Gun Emporium

Bang-Bang-Bang! Lunderon strikes Leeken's door with his dark blue Tiban crystal-topped ebonised walking stick crying. "Open up, Boldonian. I do not wish to stand here like a common passer-by." His scarred beak and missing eye make him look seriously sinister. He lost the eye to a Blue Silvenex he was hunting. The creature almost had him. Its claw sliced through his eye before he shot it in the head with a point-four pistol. He could have the eye easily repaired, but he likes its sinister look, and the advantage the unseen biomechanical eye beneath the eyepatch gives him. It can electronically connect with any weapon that he uses. Effectively becoming a heads-up display or HUD. Giving him all the advantages of a sophisticated targeting and tracking system. He had the eye patch made from a section of the dead Silvenexian's carapace, and to ensure something like that would not happen again, he increased his personal shield to the highest that can be manufactured for personal use which is a point-eight.

Leeken's face appears on the door's view screen. Only years of dealing with the arrogant Anunnaki stops him from showing his displeasure. He unlatches the magnetic lock and Lunderon strides in. Two cowed Thibrans on his heels.

Lunderon points his walking stick directly at Leeken's head growling, "It had better be ready, Gunsmith."

Leeken eyes the Tiban crystal wearily. He is not sure if his point-eight personal shield will protect him from the blast of energy that the Tiban weapon system can deliver. Lunderon is different from most Anunnaki. His brag-bag computer is housed in a walking stick, hosting the same shield technology, and recording computer, but with an ultra-powerful Tiban crystal weapon system mounted on its top.

"It's ready, Lunderon, and has been for several days. I contacted your people last week saying it was ready for inspection and testing."

Lunderon's Green and Blue plumage along his head flares up in a display of anger. Wack! The luckless Thibran standing next to him gets smacked with the heavy-topped walking stick. "Why was I not informed of this?" The arrogant, cruel hunter snarls. The Thibran is cowering on the floor holding his bleeding head, whimpering pitifully. The other is standing holding a grav-plate carrier with wide eyes, shaking slightly. "We will talk of this later." The two Thibrans tremble in fear. They have heard that tone of voice before.

"My rifle, Gunsmith? Where is it? Must I wait here forever in your dank premises?" Sneers Lunderon.

Leeken just points towards the gun range and walks out from behind his counter. He is too angry to speak.

Lunderon walks arrogantly after him. The click of his walking stick counting off his paces.

Sitting on a cloth-covered table is a sleek tri-barrelled rifle. Each barrel is slightly wider than its neighbour.

"Explain your work, Gunsmith…Is it as I ordered?"

Leeken picks up the rifle and quickly dismantles it. It only has five parts and weighs four pounds.

"As per your instructions. The battery tube fits into the rifle's buttstock and is easily and quickly changeable." Leeken removes and refits the green-striped battery to demonstrate. "The extra weight of the battery helps with the balance of the weapon. The trigger assembly and hard-light activator in the receiver are all one piece. The triple barrel rotates by hand or by pushing the button beside the trigger guard or through the linked HUD specifications you gave me for your biomechanical eye. Without the HUD, the receiver section has a mounting rail for a multi-function sighting system as you requested. Each barrel is removable for servicing." He pulls each barrel to demonstrate. "Barrel one is a point-three. Barrel two is a point-four, and barrel three is a point-five." Leeken rebuilds the weapon, makes it safe and hands it to Lunderon.

Lunderon snatches the weapon from Leeken's hand and primes it. Rotating the barrels for the point-three position, he fires off several shots at a target, twenty yards away. The centre section of the target is one big hole. He rotates the barrels to the point-four position and fires off another half a dozen pulses. The target has a new tight group of slightly larger holes in it. He rotates the weapon to the final barrel position and fires a single shot with the point-five. The target disintegrates. Changing his aim to a new target, he fires the point-five again. The entire centre of that target is gone. Lunderon gives a small grunt of pleasure then throws the rifle back to Leeken; only exceptionally good reflexes stop it from landing on the floor.

With a sniff, Lunderon sneers saying, "The trigger pull is too tight, and the spacing of the butt is too long. It does not sit against my beak properly; have these modifications done at once. I will return in two hours. Make sure everything is to my specifications." Lifting up his walking stick, he points it at Leeken's face, snarling, "Or else, I will see your paltry shop is banned from the Anunnaki Hunting Society's list of providers. Don't fail me, Gunsmith."

Lunderon kicks his Thibrans to get them moving out of the way and strides arrogantly out of Leeken's gun-shop.

"What a piece of Gromal shit!" Leeken grumbles to himself. Then a sly grin slides across his face. He quickly takes the rifle into his workshop and strips it down, completing the modifications in no time at all. Fitting the little device into each barrel took a bit longer. Leeken smiles maliciously at his work. The arrogant piece of Gromal shit will not threaten him again. That's for sure. He now has the ability to make the barrels explode if the weapon is ever pointed at him again.

Two hours on the dot, and in strides Lunderon. He grabs the rifle from Leeken's hand and checks Leeken's work. The trigger is perfect and his beak rests comfortably in the hollowed-out section of the buttstock. He grunts his approval and passes his wrist computer under Leeken's Money Transference Scanner (MTS); with a soft ping, the money is automatically transferred to Leeken's account.

With no goodbye or thank you, Lunderon arrogantly strides out of the shop. His two Thibrans follow behind with the rifle on a grav-plate carrier, heading back to a nearby berth in the spaceport where his converted Anunnaki Harvester Scoutcraft sits on its landing legs.

Leeken sits with a puzzled look on his face. This arrogant scaletick is the fifth Anunnaki hunter who's been stocking up on new gear or getting weapons serviced. There must be a new hunting venue coming up someplace. He will need to check it out. If it's big enough, he might go there and offer his services as an on-the-spot gunsmith. Bringing a selection of his stock with him for eager buyers to peruse. He is a Boldonian, after all, and he will make a profit, or his name is not Leeken Va-D. Praise be to commerce.

# Thera Three
# Present Day

Stex Va-D stands in front of his newly constructed warehouse rubbing his hands together. This venture had turned from a catastrophe into an exceptionally good little money spinner. The latest bulk freighter had just docked with the orbital warehouse that houses all of his stock. He will have his sales team check for shortages and top up any empty shelves. He's been informed by one of Anibuna's minions that a new enterprise is coming soon, and he will need the Boldonian to supply it with all the consumables it may require. Food, drink, hunting paraphernalia, ammunition, and phase gun batteries. Stex wonders if his cousin Leeken would be interested in this. He will need to give him a call.

Stex Va-D's Shop is more like an all-purpose money-stripping unit. Anything Stex can come up with to fill his tills is fair game. The front section of his shopping complex has been converted into a bar-come restaurant and caters to the off-duty Andrend Poltox and any Anunnaki who wander by. Plenty of purple ale and food is available. Courtesy of the six replicators he had fitted into his kitchen, he also has supplies of Wooggi sent in from the Poltox planetary system on a regular basis to offer to his customers, at a price, of course.

# Anibuna Ninety-Nines, Thera Three Safari Experience

In a massive advertising blitz throughout the Anunnaki worlds, Anibuna's Safari Experience is launched. The fancy headlines in the infomercials and the beautiful video footage of a predominately water-covered Thera Three draw in the crowds. No other world in Anunnaki space has as much water. The slick marketing then shows the introduced game animals getting dropped off in the Australian outback. The Conpex immediately start to chase down the odd-looking local wildlife. These creatures with huge rear legs and long strong-looking tails bound away from the ravenous Conpex and out of the camera's view.

Then his prize attraction. The Adamu flash onto the screen. Every Anunnaki who ever went to the Games knew about the famous Romans of old, and the recent introduction of the Marines had started to whet appetites. These are the types of Adamu that the hunters are being told they will face. Touted to be elusive and dangerous adversaries that would require only the best hunters to be able to take one down. Footage of the Romans and Marines fighting in the Games is played to display their marital prowess.

The booking line for the initial places is swamped within hours. A cap of one thousand hunters per safari is introduced so the individual hunters have room to move without any chance of two hunters stalking the same game. This capping of the numbers just puts the prices up even higher. With hunters willing to pay above the asking price to be able to brag they were the first hunters on-site.

The savvy Anibuna decides to do a one-off special event. A five-day inaugural hunt.

This will be for twenty hunters only, and these will be specially selected from the big-name celebrity hunters throughout the Anunnaki clans. The ticket prices for this one-off event are obscenely high.

The inaugural hunt is set for the following week. Individual hunting reserves have been laid out specifically to give each hunter a virgin area to conduct his own hunt. There is no bag limit, and there is nothing that cannot be hunted.

North America is sectioned into four areas: north, south, east, and west.

South America gets split into four as well; one being the heavily jungled Amazon.

Japan gets her own hunter to scour this area individually.

India is split in two.

Europe is quartered, again north, south, east, and west.

Scotland gets a single hunter.

Mexico gets the last four and is quartered the same as the rest.

Luxury houses in each area have replicators installed which will cater for any food other than what they will eat from their kills and will act as a base for each hunter and his entourage of Thibrans and collared hunting dogs of Blue or Black Silvenex.

The last of the Koban dinosaurs had died off months ago. The electricity is flowing again. Electronic equipment all works as before. People start to come up out of the holes and deep shelters where they had successfully hidden themselves and their families. Is the nightmare finally showing some signs of lifting…Hell no! Things are about to get much worse.

# Lunderon

Lunderon is descended from Anunnaki royalty. He can trace his clan; the Anisol, back to the original home planet Anun. He was hatched into a very wealthy clan of totally ruthless slavers that built their empire on the backs of captured beings from various nearby worlds. It was the Anisol Anunnaki that had invaded Thibra and enslaved the entire planet. The gentle timid Thibrans put up no resistance at all. The introduction of the pain-inducing slave collars invented by the Anisol insured the poor Thibrans did whatever their new masters the Anunnaki desired.

Taking the planet Thibra for their own use, the Anisol clan leave a token force on Anun and establish their new slaving empire renaming Thibra as Ospan. The Ospan tree on Anun produces delicious fruit all year round. If it's fed and trimmed, it gives succulent fruit for ever. From Ospan, they supply the rest of the Anunnaki clans with the Thibrans as slaves. The Thibrans breed at a prodigious rate, so the Anisol Anunnaki find themselves on a planet full of slaves that constantly renew themselves. They only sell male slaves, and they are neutered to stop the buyers from just breeding their own stock. Thibrans become the favoured servants of the Anunnaki.

The Anisol stopped dealing with any other form of slaves and concentrated on training the pliable Thibrans to undertake any task required of them to please their new masters the Anunnaki.

This is the world Lunderon is hatched into. Safe, secure, and as boring as hell. The hatchling Lunderon craves excitement. A nearby moon with an atmosphere holds some ferocious predators. He and four of his friends go on a hunt. Two days later, a badly mauled Lunderon is the only one of them to return. His father, Rahainon, the clan leader of the Anisol is furious. Not at the fact his offspring had been injured or that the others were killed and eaten, but the fact he had failed. It's just as well the hatchling had not received his brag-bag at that point. The early recorded failure would have been too much of a stain on the family's name. Lunderon would have been killed to preserve the Anisol clan's status.

Lunderon's injuries are healed, but the scar across his beak by order of his father is retained as a reminder of his failure.

A famous Poltox mercenary turned big game hunter is contracted to teach the hatchling Anunnaki the secrets of hunting game or anything else for that matter, using a variety of weapons and traps.

Lunderon is an exemplary student. Within five years, he has surpassed the Poltox in cunning and field craft. The old Poltox had been injured during one of their hunts and had a foot torn up so bad the auto-doc could not fully repair it. The Poltox started to use a sturdy walking stick as an aid onto which he had cleverly mounted a point two-phase pistol. Lunderon loved it.

The day of Lunderon's brag-bag ceremony where it's deemed that he is old enough that his actions will now be recorded, and he can now rise or fall in Anisol society by his own actions has come. Flouting the standard handheld bag as his recorder. He has his fitted into a walking stick.

The walking stick incorporates his recording computer and a point-four personal shield. This all fits neatly into the shaft of the stick.

A point-two phase pistol is artistically formed into the walking stick's handle. It's in the shape of a miniature Conpex skull to remind him of the beast that slashed his beak.

Everyone thought this to be too radical. Lunderon thought it set him apart from the herd, and he intended to be well in front of them all. As the years pass and technology progresses, he modifies his walking stick repeatedly, eventually finding a Tiban crystal which when weaponised makes a phase pistol look like a hatchling toy.

# Thera Three, Anibuna's Mansion Madera

Anibuna stands stunned before his communications console. The confused face of Petral's aide Malfee stares at him in wonder.

"Do you wish me to repeat the message, My Lord?"

Anibuna just nods.

"By the grace of our clan leader Petral Seven. Because of the abundance of congratulations that has flooded into this office regarding your idea of turning Thera Three into a hunting reserve. He has elevated your status from ninety-nine to ninety. Congratulations, Anibuna Ninety. Signed Petral Seven."

Anibuna is still too stunned to speak. He just nods graciously.

"Farewell, sir, and again congratulations." …The screen returns to its base setting showing the Gishma clan's eagle.

Anibuna screams out to his Thibrans to bring him some wine and a bowl of the little scurrying creatures they found in the cellar with the long tails. They're delicious. He stands and does a happy dance in the middle of the room. Flaring out his wings, he screams, "Ninety!"

# Thera Three Spaceport Azores Islands

The Azores was missed by the dinosaurs. Over the months, it received thousands of refugees putting the island under great strain food-wise, but with clever use of the fertile land and plenty of eager helpers, food is being produced to keep the population fed. The horror stories coming in over the radio are frightening. The large spaceship that hovered over the centre of the islands many months later is downright terrifying. A massive green flash in the sky takes away all their fears as every human and animal on the island falls afoul of the Anunnaki slaver's incapacitator pulse.

Holding domes are constructed to float on the twin lakes in the Sete Cidades Massif Caldera and a small army of Thibrans load almost one hundred and fifty thousand cryogenically frozen humans into the green-tinted domes, secure for whatever the Anunnaki have in store for them.

A spaceport is constructed beside the island's existing airport, and in record time, there is a constant back-and-forth shuttling of craft from orbit to the flourishing port. The Belatan Occupation Force quickly used this as a staging area shuttling Andrend mercenaries to various existing military bases throughout the planet. The Poltox modify existing airports to be able to handle their dropships. Soon there are Poltox barracks spread throughout the planet. Each commandeered military base or spaceport holds a brood group of Andrend Poltox.

The Azores Spaceport is chosen as a central location for the inaugural hunt. The Games Galactivision Unit is set up to capture this historic new venture. Anibuna Ninety preens in front of the camera as a shuttle brings down the hunters. The Games hosts and commentators are glad to be back in business after the unexpected closure of the Yonath Games. They eagerly await the chance to interview the top twenty hunters in all of Anunnaki space.

The door of the shuttle slides open and a ramp folds down to the concrete surface of the runway. Out walk the hunters, resplendent in their colourful feathers and matching hunter's harnesses.

The Games Galactivision host Sparyten whose face is well-known throughout Anunnaki space speaks directly into the camera. His pink and green feathers are groomed and shining under the camera's lights. He starts off with his trademark stretched-out first line…

"Annnd. Here we go, Games fans. First down the ramp for this inaugural hunt is someone I don't need to tell you; our number one hunter, who never comes back with an empty bag. Gentle Beings…Lunderon of the Anisol."

Lunderon looks directly at the camera and gives a curt nod, then enters the plush transporter that is waiting to take them to the staging area for the start of the hunt.

"Next down the ramp is Ofintin of the Padenon." The Pink and green feathered hunter waves towards the camera. "Following him is Coli and Linn of the Holinda." Their yellow and red plumage glistens in the sun as they wave towards the camera.

"And now we see Holentin of the Padenon. Famous for his fight last year with a Janark in the Games."

Holentin waves his brag-bag above his head and walks down the ramp.

Sparyten claps his fellow Padenon on the back as he passes. "Top of the ramp, we now have Rankill and Cronn of the Hitori. New to the Games, but renowned hunters in Hitori space. A big welcome to you both." The blue and yellow feathered hunters wave frantically at the camera.

"And no introductions needed here, Games lovers… Hipsips of the Idonax. Top hunter in the Idonax quadrant."

The red and black feathered Hipsips lifts his hand and gives his trademark wave with one finger held up above his left shoulder.

Sparyten laughs and says, "Yes, still number one. Another relatively newcomer to the Games' top twenty, we have Inipan of the Anisol. A graduate of the famous Lunderon Hunting School."

Inipan gives a curt nod same as his idol Lunderon.

"Oh! Gentle beings, a great trio who often hunt together. Cumlox, Oxinter and Pulixef of the Gishma."

A little group of Thibrans at the bottom of the ramp do a happy dance and clap their hands as their masters stride confidently down the ramp.

"Ah, gentle beings, another fine pair. No strangers to the Games. Ikell and Potts of the Holinda."

Both yellow and red-plumed hunters give a cheery wave, slapping each other on the back they bound down the ramp and into the transport.

"Annnd, our next duo is Nixmal and Pzull of the Hitori. Famous for their kill rate in past Games when they faced the dreaded Limies. What was it? Twenty a second?" Pzull holds up three fingers.

"That's right, thirty! Thirty Limies a second! Fantastic. Good luck to you both."

The blue and yellow feathered pair give a jaunty wave and walk down to the transport. On their heels, the next pair of intrepid hunters come into view.

"Lorrt and Hinpat of the Idonax, Gentle Beings. Always great value."

The two red and black feathered Idonax Anunnaki give a wave and troop onto the transporter.

"Annnd our last pair, gentle beings. Extopp and Bartex of the Gishma."

The little group of Thibrans do their happy dance again as their masters walk arrogantly towards the waiting transport. The doors close and the transport lifts on its repulsors and glides off to the holding area where their individual hunting licences and weaponry are waiting for their eager hands.

Sparyten looks seriously into the camera and says, "We hand you over now to our resident expert who is at the staging area from where the hunters will head out to their individual hunting areas…Over to you, Rametunn."

The screen swiftly changes to the interior of a large dome. It is sectioned off into twenty areas that are a hive of activity with Thibrans scurrying about with boxes and crates of hunting gear. In one corner are cages holding the Silvenex slave 'hunting dogs'.

Holding his hand up to his ear slot, the red and black feathered Rametunn looks directly into the camera with a serious expression on his face and starts his spiel.

"I can tell you this, gentle beings, the hunters today have it easy. Back in my day, it was just you, your rifle, and a dozen or so Thibrans. Today's hunters are spoiled by the technology they bring with them. Look at this!" The camera points to one of the hunter's booths. On the bench is a plethora of sophisticated equipment.

"Tracking drones, motion sensors, pheromone detectors, green light incapacitator pulse generators, spring traps. It's obvious, this hunter does not have a Black or Blue hunting dog. We will check them out later as they go on show to see which is best of breed."

His hand goes back up to his ear again. "Ah, gentle beings, the transporter's just pulled up to the dome. And yes, here come the contestants. I can see many old faces I have hunted against, and it's good to see some fresh blood being brought into the hunt."

The camera swings round to catch the hunters looking around to find their individual slots. Thibrans jog up to their masters to guide them to their areas. Good-humoured insults fly from some of the older hunters as they settle into their booths and start prepping their gear.

Lunderon ignores his equipment. He knows his Thibrans will have it all set up to his exact specifications, or else they would follow the fate of the two unfortunates who had not informed him his rifle was ready. He had them liquified as food for his matched pair of Silvenex. One Blue and one Black. Both of these poor creatures are so broken that they have virtually no will of their own anymore. Their stingers and mandibles have been removed and their bodies have been dyed a vivid green with his family crest burnt into their thorax and painted with liquid gold. His pair won best of breed most times they went on the show. His Silvenex can no longer inject the enzyme that liquifies their food and relies entirely on Lunderon doing this for them. He studies the Games board to see which hunting area he has been allocated.

On a wall is a huge map of the planet. It's been divided up into twenty individual hunting reserves. His name sits over Japan. Walking over to the administration booth, he collects his licence and information pack telling him about his hunting reserve. Reading it, he sees that fifteen Conpex had been dropped into the area two days ago along with four Janarks and two Nomals. There are still some wild Adamu on the islands it seems, and these are marked as being extremely dangerous. Lunderon is looking forward to hunting these things for the first time. He arrogantly walks over to his booth and prepares to start his hunt.

In the background is a line of ten polished silver metal cages just big enough for a Silvenex to stand upright in it. Several judges walk up and down examining the polished and perfectly displayed 'hunting dogs.' There are six Black and four Blue Silvenex. Lunderon is the only hunter with two.

The judges come to their conclusion. Lunderon wins the title again. Gentle applause greets the result.

The destroyed minds of the Silvenex just look out dully from the cages. They don't move a muscle for fear of the modified multi-crystal imbedded collars terrifyingly severe lash.

Each hunter is allowed a personal skimmer with a towed equipment trailer and twelve Thibrans that act as beaters and serve their Anunnaki master while he is 'roughing it.' The Thibrans travel in the trailer along with the rest of his property.

Each hunter receives his allocated hunting reserve, and they board transports to be flown out to begin the hunt. The hunt begins as soon as they reach their designated area.

The first to reach his hunting reserve is Ofintin of the Padenon. He has chosen to land in Spain as it has two of his wishlist kills there. A Janark and a Nomal. He collects heads and has a special enzyme formula which when injected into the flesh preserves it. The heads are then tastefully mounted and added to his collection. He usually eats the rest of the body.

He lands with his twelve Thibrans and they set up camp. The first thing Ofintin does is launch several drones to search the area for signs of his prey. He has never been comfortable with Silvenex. No matter how well-trained they are. So, he doesn't use them. The drones silently streak away in all directions. Two Thibrans sit glued to multiple screens showing the drone's telemetry and video feeds. While he is waiting, Ofintin walks down to the beach and stares out into the water. He has never seen so much of it in his long life. He wades into the pleasantly warm water. Lifting up a handful, he sniffs it. Salty he thinks. Sticking his tongue into the small pool of liquid in his palm, he tastes it, yep, extremely salty. Tastes great. He dips his beak into the water and drinks down great gulps of the spectacularly good water.

The reptilians have a special absorption system in their bodies. Developed over aeons to enable them to survive on the predominantly dry worlds found in the rest of the quadrant. They need to be able to consume any type of liquid or water in order to survive. His thoughts are brought back to the present by one of his Thibrans as it calls out they have a contact.

Drone five has picked up movement. It circles silently two hundred feet above the target.

Below the drone, a Conpex is stalking prey.

Julio Lopez watches through a slot in the metal door as one of the dreaded Diablo Dinosaurio comes stalking into the village. He has not seen one of these pesadillas for months. His daughter Maria who is only five starts to scream. The Conpex's head swivels quickly towards the sound. It's at the door in two massive bounds and is furiously scratching at it. Maria is screaming her lungs out. Julio quickly picks up his daughter and heads for the wine cellar they have been using as a sanctuary for almost a year.

The drone is six miles away. Ofintin grabs his rifle and a Thibran then jumps on his skimmer and slams the throttle wide open. He is there in under a minute. He parks the skimmer two houses over from where the Conpex is still snarling and scratching at a door. Sliding his custom-made point-four rifle from its sheath, he calmly takes aim. He does not want to damage the skull. So, he aims for an area just below its neck intending to sever its spinal cord, killing it instantly.

The Conpex has just torn the door from its hinges when the light hum of the shot drops it like a puppet with its strings cut. The pulse of hard light goes straight through its neck and blows out a section of the door frame. Ofintin walks forward to examine his kill. He stops short when he hears the cries of some creature in the dwelling. Opening one of the many pouches on his hunter's harness, he pulls out a small blue sphere. Pushing a button on its top, he throws it into the house just as Julio looks out of the cellar door to see if the Dinosaurio has gone. The flash of green light from the incapacitator grenade is the last thing he will ever see, and be able to do anything about

Ofintin shoulders his rifle and pulls out a point-two pistol. He cautiously enters the building covering all the corners with the pistol. Lying half-way out of the cellar door is Julio and just behind him are his wife and daughter. Ofintin gives the air a good rendition of his hunter's victory cry. He has just bagged his first Adamu without even trying, and this is just day one. He orders his Thibrans to collect his trophies and bring them down to the beach.

He injects all four of his kills. Well, technically, the Adamu are still alive. Being under the green light's influence, they won't feel a thing. He thought himself to be a considerate hunter and never made his prey suffer if he could help it. The injections take thirty minutes to fully preserve his trophies. No prize had ever come back and told him it was excruciatingly painful for every second until the trophies were preserved.

Using a laz-blade, he removes the head of the Conpex in one clean straight cut. He then goes through the capping rings in his trophy kit until he finds one that neatly fits around the stump. Once fitted, he pushes a green section of the cap, and it shrinks to fit exactly around the neck, sealing it permanently and finishing off the trophy with a neat and tidy base. It's now ready to be put into his collection. The Lopez family watch the whole thing from frozen but seeing eyes. They are all screaming silently in terror, unable to move a muscle.

Thankfully, the enzymes kill them before Ofintin carefully removes their heads.

"Annnd there we have it, gentle beings. The first kill of Anibuna's inaugural hunt goes to Ofintin of the Padenon. Well done, Ofintin. A commemorative plaque will be waiting for you on the last day of the hunt. Stay tuned, gentle beings. Highlights of the action are available on our pay-for-view channel four. Contact your local Games outlet for details."

Lunderon dismisses the news. He has just landed outside Osaka after completing several sweeps of the islands with his ship's scanners. He knows roughly where the animals are and has a couple of locations for the elusive Adamu. All is ready. He is prepping his camp site when a high-velocity projectile smacks into the side of his head. His inbuilt ballistics tracer in his bionic eye has already traced the projectile's back path and has it coming from a high building nearly a quarter of a mile away. Impressive. He is up against another hunter...An Adamu hunter.

He gives a wide grin, opening his beak and sticking his tongue out. This is more like it. A second impact slams into his personal shield hitting almost the same spot. He traces it back to the same window at the top of a building a quarter of a mile away. Lunderon does not move an inch. The projectile's impact is easily absorbed by his point-eight personal shield. For all his fame as a hunter, losing his eye to the Silvenex all that time ago effected his confidence. Since then, he has taken no chances. So, thinking to himself, he says, "*Why have a dog and bark yourself!*" He presses a button on his walking stick. His Blue Silvenexians cage springs open.

"Here," growls Lunderon.

The Silvenex is at his side in seconds.

"The building with the red roof. Top floor, second window from this side. Capture the Adamu that's there and bring it to me. Retrieve its weapon and any gear it has on-site. Go."

The Silvenex darts off towards the building.

Sargent Akio Tanaka has lived by his wits since the madness of the dinosaurs and the invasion of the North Koreans which had ended about seven months earlier. The slaughter of the JDF (Japanese Defence Force) by the dinosaurs and the futuristically armed North Koreans was almost total. Once the North Koreans had swept across the length of Japan devastating most of the armed forces and civilians that they could find, they reboarded the cargo vessels that had brought them over and returned to the mainland. There were a lot of dinosaurs left as a mopping-up force, but a few months ago, they all mysteriously died. Then miraculously, a few weeks after that, the electricity and electronics came back on. A small contingent of the JDF had been held back to try and defend the remaining civilians. It was from that unit that Tanaka had come.

People had started to come up to the surface thinking the horror was finally coming to an end. His unit had hidden deep underground in Osaka's railway tunnels only coming to the surface three months ago. Since then, the JDF has been trying to bring some semblance of order back to the country. People have been living in the underground railway tunnels for too long and are desperate to get back to the surface. Now what is this new thing that has landed? He is told that a spaceship has landed in Kyobashi Park. He treks from his base camp in Kyobashi railway station in the middle of Osaka to see what this thing is.

Tanaka watches the spaceship disgorge several small aliens that scurry about unloading equipment of some kind. Then down the ramp walks a large green and blue feathered alien. It looks like a bird-man. Not willing to take a chance, Akio quickly sets up in the post office just across from the park and adjusts his scope for roughly four hundred and fifty yards. Taking a calming breath, he gently squeezes the trigger and puts a bullet into the side of its green and blue feathered birdlike head...To no effect whatsoever.

Stunned at the result, Akio quickly re-aims and shoots again. The thing did not even flinch. Akio in a panic relocates. He does not see the Silvenex streak towards his building.

Ouyden can barely remember her name but can still feel a slight pity for the creature she is about to capture. With a flick of her wrist, she throws the net of the web she had spun over the Adamu as she had been told they were called and pulls tight. Akio struggles and curses but to no avail. The steel strong ultra-fine webbing entangles the Adamu. She knocks him to the ground and then gathers up all the equipment that's beside the fallen sniper. With a strength well above what you would expect from her frail-looking body, she lifts the Adamu plus his gear and walks back to Lunderon.; Akio kicking and screaming the entire way.

Lunderon stands arrogantly tapping his foot with impatience on the concrete pavement as Ouyden approaches.

"What took you so long?" A split second's pulse of pain rips through Ouyden. She drops to one knee in pain letting out a hiss and lowers the sniper at Lunderon's feet along with his rifle and pack.

Ignoring the struggling screaming Adamu, Lunderon picks up Akio's rifle. It's a 7.62 M24 SWS.

He inspects the rifle admiring its sleek metal and if he is not mistaken, wooden framework. A cursory glance shows him where the priming lever and safety are. He lifts the weapon to his shoulder and looks down the scope at a streetlight about a quarter of a mile away. He lines up the crosshairs and squeezes the trigger. The recoil takes him by surprise. The shot misses by a wide margin. He grunts in surprise. Looking at the rifle again, it is obvious that it fires a projectile at a fairly high velocity, but it is subject to the forces acting upon it. He aims again using his own HUD to align the sight. He notices looking at the original sight cross hairs that his aim point is well above where he is aiming. Ballistic curve he thinks to himself and squeezes the trigger again. The streetlight shatters. He gives a little grunt of satisfaction and puts the gun aside. He will add it to his collection of weapons taken from beings who had tried to kill him over the years. Searching through Akio's pack and combat harness, he finds six magazines, each holding five bullets.

The ultimate hunt. Hunter versus hunter.

He calmly inspects the Adamu. Working out which finger would have been the trigger finger. Then with callous disregard, he shoots the Adamu in the head with his handgun.

"Remove it from the web then return to your cage." Ouyden does so quickly so as not to receive another stroke of the lash.

Lunderon bends down and removes the sniper's trigger finger which he puts into a cryo-pouch to preserve it. He will have it treated and mounted before it goes into his collection.

A good start.

# Andrend Maxus Brood
# Commander Fedoon Belatan
# Peacekeeping Force

Fedoon stares hard at the view screen. Wishing he were within claw range of the arrogant scaleslime that is sneering safely into his camera pick-up somewhere on the surface of Thera Three.

"Mercenary commander. Order your mercenaries to stay clear of the hunters that are on the planet at this time. We would not want an accident to happen where one of your brood is mistaken for a wild animal," sneers Doplon.

"They would only do it once, Anunnaki. They would only do it once. Then you would see a real hunt."

"Watch your tongue, mercenary. That sounded too much like a threat."

"No. No threat, Anunnaki. None whatsoever. It was a statement of fact. My brood mates have already been told to stay away from your pampered so-called hunters. We're more worried about being shot by incompetent amateurs who barely know which end of the stick they hold emits the hard light. So, fear not, Anunnaki. Unless we get word from our Belatan employers to interfere with your 'Games', you can play with your toys all you like. Now any further communications about my brood mates you make through Senior Judge Durnesson on the ship."

Click!

Doplon stares at a blank screen. He has been hung-up on! By a mere employee no less. His arrogance demands a reprisal. His crown crest flares up in anger displaying the red feathers under the purple outer ones. He immediately calls Senior Judge Durnesson to complain.

"Durnesson, one of your mercenaries threatened and insulted me. I demand he be punished to the limit of your power," sneers Doplon, staring into his comms screen.

The wheezing chuffing sound of Durnesson's laughter stops Doplon dead.

"Oh my, my, my, Doplon. You have no idea of the Poltox whatsoever, do you?" On-screen, the large iguana-like head shakes from side to side. "I was standing beside *Prince* Fedoon when he answered your call. You didn't even know his name. Did you?" Another sad shake of his head. "The arrogance of your race will eventually cause you all severe problems. So, back to your rather hatchling-like rant. No! I will not discipline a much-regarded prince of one of the most powerful Poltox Clans in the system."

"Now listen carefully, Doplon. The Belatan Government will honour the findings of the Supreme Court regarding Thera Three. *If,* it stays legally binding. Randor has put in an injunction regarding the legality of the case and is preparing a counter action as I speak. You better hope all your facts in this case are airtight, Doplon. Otherwise, you may see just how effective Poltox can be."

Doplon's screen goes blank for a second time without his input. Furious, he cries out but calms down as he thinks of his latest venture. He needs to call Anibuna and tell him of his successful tests.

Anibuna stares at the screen as it flashes showing an incoming call with Doplon's name beside it.

He activates the screen and growls, his crest rising slightly in displeasure. "Yes, Doplon, what is it? I am extremely busy with the hunt."

Doplon is about to tell Anibuna about his successful test when Anibuna asks him to ready the Adamu soldiers to be used as game animals once the hunts start for real. Very soon.

Doplon tells Anibuna that the soldiers in the domes have been sent up to Eden Base by order of Joadin for experimentation purposes.

Anibuna is shocked into silence. His main hunting attractions are off the planet. What in the two hells is Joadin thinking? Has his number one status gone to his head?

"Why would he do that? It makes no sense at all. It was Joadin who suggested we keep them in the domes prior to selling them to the Games. No money was lost in feeding them or hiring guards to keep them from making mischief. He stood to make a fortune, along with every other Gishma on Thera Three as we split the slave sales."

"I don't know, sir. He never mentioned anything other than he wanted plenty of test subjects as his techniques would use up many of them during his experimentation."

"What experiments? He has the Adamex fine-tuned and perfect. It's what got him his number one slot after all."

"I don't know, sir. He usually confides in me, but he has been quiet lately."

"What is it you wanted to see me about anyway, Doplon?"

"I have perfected my scanner, sir. I have tested it myself on several of my Thibrans that I had subsumed local Thera Three animals. It works perfectly. The scanners picked out my Thibrans from a herd of the local four-legged animals that can be found in the forest."

"What scanner? You scientists and your scaleticked secrets."

"I can detect a shapeshifted being." His head plume rises up in pride. "The security applications of this when sold on the open market will make us a fortune."

The biggest fear of all shapeshifting societies is detecting an infiltrator trying to enter their planets or colonies for nefarious reasons. These are almost impossible to detect when the individual has all the memories and skills of its host to seamlessly merge into its targeted population.

Extremely good pheromone receptors in some beings, like the Black Silvenex can pick it up, and voice recognition software can detect that the voice is not quite a match to its holder, but it is not one hundred per cent accurate. So, a guaranteed scanner at border posts or spaceport terminals would be worth a fortune to virtually every government galaxy-wide.

"Well, that is interesting. Well done, Doplon. Is your scanner fixed or mobile?"

"It can be both, sir. The unit itself is not much bigger than a pulse pistol."

"Let's test it on the hunters and see what happens. It will be interesting to see if we have any cheats, and I have just the very thing to deal with cheats." He strides over to the special radio that is linked to his Blue Silvenex and calls them.

"Silvenex, where are you? Stop what you are doing. Terminate the remaining female Koban. I have no further use for them. Bring me their heads as a trophy. Make your way to the nearest Belatan outpost. I will tell them you will be eliminating the last of the Koban threat, so you will receive their assistance if it is required. Do not fail me in front of those arrogant mercenaries. Once you have completed your task, I will secure transport for you to be brought to my island. Do you understand, Silvenex?"

"Yes, Master Anibuna it will be done." The receiver goes silent. "Arrogant web-snarled, carapace licker," snarls Joaxona, vowing to herself to end his life one day in a slow and terrible way.

She calls out to Zin and Ohna that she and her sisters may have a way into the heart of the Anunnaki enterprise on Earth, and as a bonus, the elimination of the last Koban.

# North Korea

Kang Kun-Mo and Yon Song-Choi aka Gigi and Lola are now the official leaders of the now Unified Korea. A spiel had been made up explaining that Kim Jong-Un the Supreme Leader is still in America with an army that's taking over the country in the name of the Korean People, and his deputies Kang Kun-Mo and Yon Song-Choi should be obeyed as if it were him giving the orders. The fanatical brainwashed Northern Korean crowds go nuts.

With the removal of the suppression web, all of South Korea's electronics and manufacturing base is working again, and the North Koreans have their southern slave workforce to make it all work for them. Now that the Koban are running things, they are in their element. Safe, secure, and with a food source the two of them can choose from any time they like, plus a culture that worships them like gods. The pair move into Kim Jong-Un's palatial mansion in the Ryongsong district and are living like queens of old.

# Eden Base Control Room

"Whatever we do on Earth has to be done in complete secrecy. If the Belatan Occupation Force finds out, we are done. There is no way we can compete with a Belatan battleship, or that Gishma crafts weaponry. Whatever we do has to be clandestine. So, we will need to use the SRCs for any actions we take on the surface." Zin walks over to Joaxona putting his hand on her shoulder. "How do you want to play this, Joaxona? We don't want you taking any unnecessary risks."

"Scarlet may want to go help her cousins. I will ask them if they want my help. I am family, after all."

Her grin is one of pure evil.

# Tokyo
# Japan

Lunderon has moved north. His drones have picked up one of the Nomals wandering through the streets of Tokyo. It has been attacked by Adamu, so he will have another chance to get an Adamu trophy. He wants a head, but first wants a crack at the Nomal. He has never hunted one of these before and is looking forward to it. He slips his walking stick into a purpose-built sheath that's in a sling over his shoulder. The activation stud for the Tiban crystal weapon in easy to reach. Halting his Thibrans who huddle into a frightened tight group, he stalks forward towards the snuffling Nomal that is midway down the street in front of him. Its broad nose is hoovering across the ground looking for prey. It suddenly becomes frantic as it paws at the ground with sharp claws digging up the concrete around a doorway. Screams can be heard from the Adamu it uncovered from its hiding place. These suddenly stop.

Lunderon watches two legs still kicking slightly protruding from its mouth as the tiny teeth shred the victim into small chunks that get swallowed with a back flick of its large flat head. The legs disappear into the meatgrinder of a mouth. Lunderon lifts his tri-barrelled rifle and selects the point-five position and single shot. Lining the cross-haired styled sight with the creature's left eye, he squeezes the trigger.

Downrange, the great beast drops onto its belly. Dead before it hit the ground. He orders his Thibrans to go forward and remove the Nomal's head and then secure it in a transport pack which will preserve it until he is ready to have it professionally mounted. He also has them slice up its delicate underside for meat. He is ravenous after the hunt; he may even allow the Thibrans to have some as well.

"Annnd. Here we go, Games fans." Sparyten's trademark grin fills the screen. "We have our first elimination of a hunter. This happened this morning. They all knew the risks and signed the waiver clearing Anibuna Nineties' inaugural hunt of any criminal charges relating to a hunter being injured or killed in the hunt. Holentin of the Padenon was killed in Scotland after falling for a trap that his prey had set up for him. Up to that point, he was doing great and had bagged two of the illusive Adamu. A full non-edited graphic video of Holentin's tragic end is available on our pay-per-view channel six. More hunt news as it happens, gentle beings. Remember the betting line is open twenty-four-seven. Pixmal of the Hitori just made a small fortune by betting that Holentin would be killed on this day. Well done, Pixmal. Collect your winnings at any Games outlet registered with the Belatan Banking Guild."

# Edinburgh
# Scotland

Holentin had his drones up for days and had not found any trace of the Adamu. He had bagged four Conpex but that was so easy as to be hatchling play for the experienced hunter. He has his Thibrans strip the bodies for meat and reduce the heads to just the skull. Two of the Thibrans are polishing them to a high gloss before they're sealed in vacuum containers. Just then, one of his drones signals it has movement. He studies the video, and there, middle of the screen are two Adamu. Selecting an overhead view, he sees they are rummaging through buildings near the water-filled area where floating vessels are tied up to stone structures.

Mary and her little sister Morag are starving. They're searching through the shops just off Leith Docks to see if they can find anything to eat. They had gotten lucky a few days ago and managed to find three cans of dog food; it was the best meal they had eaten in months. The local militia had warned them about the spaceship that had landed in nearby Murryfield Stadium a couple of days ago, but the sisters were so hungry that they ignored the advice.

Holentin stalks the sisters keeping upwind. He finds the ideal spot for a hide and sets up his rifle. He has a choice of several, but for this historic kill, he selects his point-three Sporting Special. He lines up the sight on the smaller of the two. It is sitting fiddling with something in its lap. Curious, he zooms in. It's a small representation of an Adamu. It even has the same reddish fur on its head. He zooms back out and aims for the centre of his target's body; he does not want the skull damaged. The hum of the rifle does not reach the sisters. Little Morag gets a hole blasted right through her chest. Her doll drops from lifeless fingers and lies beside her. Startled, Mary looks over wondering why Morag is lying down. She is still wondering when a second shot from Holentin tears its way towards her blasting out a great chunk of her right lung. Doing a little victory dance, he sends his Thibrans to collect his kills. Strip them of meat and remove the skulls.

George McGowan, a local militia leader watched the whole thing through binoculars. He is unable to help the poor Bairns, but he vows to them that they will be avenged. He quickly slides out of his hide and runs to the cellar where they are staying for the night. It's just off Leith Docks. He reports what he has seen.

"Christ, Geordie, what's up, man? Ye look as white as a sheet," Dougie Hamilton asks in a worried tone.

"That bastardin thing frae the spaceship just shot and skinned wee Morag and her sister Mary."

"No!"

"Aye, man, it was a hellish thing to watch. Go get the rest o' the lads. We need to kill this fucker."

"Whit ages were the lassies, Geordie?"

"Ten and six. They werny sisters, ye ken, but after their mothers were killed by the dinosaurs, they clung to each other and started calling each other sister."

"We need tae make this bastard suffer, Geordie."

"Oh, we will, man. We will."

During when the dinosaurs were tearing through Edinburgh, a clever way was found to kill them. The narrow, cobbled streets were great ambush sites, and it was found that heavy dockside chains from anchors could be suspended above these alleyways and dropped on the dinosaurs killing or trapping them until they could be killed by shooting them in the head. They will set it up for this creature. They just need to lure it into a trap.

Several of McGowan's men set up a mock camp just inside Leith Docks. There is only one approach to this through an alleyway that's been rigged with suspended chains. It's just a matter of waiting for the shite to turn up. A whispered voice over a walkie-talkie says, "Get ready. Here it comes."

Holentin stalks towards the small camp he saw on a drone feed. Just in front of him is a pile of wooden crates. They make an almost perfect hunter's hide with a clear shot of three Adamu who are huddled around a fire. They are much larger than the ones he had taken before. Grinning, he ushers his Thibrans forward. He has a perfect view of the targets. Just as George McGowan had set it up to be.

Holentin sets up his hide. Six Thibrans help him. Above him, four men with razor-sharp knives await the signal to cut the rope holding the mass of the chain.

McGowan whispers, "Now, lads."

The pile of chains falls thirty feet and smashes into Holentin and the Thibrans. The Thibrans are killed instantly. Holentin's personal shield saves his life.

Hate-filled Scots gather around the fallen bird-man. McGowan lowers his rifle until it is just six inches away from its pink and green feathered head and starts to squeeze the trigger.

Dougie Hamilton holds his hand over the receiver of McGowan's rifle pushing it gently down. "Na, Na, Geordie. Too quick, man. This shite has tae suffer." Looking around, he nods to a young man standing beside him, "Scott, go get some petrol. We will cook this fekking chicken alive."

Scott McIntyre goes and brings back a jerry can of fuel. They pour it over the creature until the can is empty. They all stand back as McGowan throws a lit match onto the pile. It seems the personal shields are not up to stopping the fire from damaging its wearer. Holentin screams and screams and screams. It did not bring back the children, but it sure as hell made the men feel better.

# Mosquerio Island
# Para Brazil

Cumlox, Pulixef and Oxinter, plus thirty-six Thibrans land on Mosquerio Island to start their hunt. Fifty Conpex had been dropped onto the seventy-four square mile island which is in the Para region of Brazil. There is reputed to be an unknown number of Adamu in the area as well. So, after hearing the news about Holentin, they are on high alert, but still in good humour. The three have been inseparable since hatching and they have an ace up their sleeve. All thirty-six of their Thibrans are armed with point-two pistols. This did not bother the trio of friends one bit. Their personal shields are point eights, and the last thing to enter their minds would be their dedicated Thibrans rebelling. That is just too ridiculous to contemplate.

The hunting camp is set up. A portable energy fence is erected by the Thibrans, and they all retreat to the safety of its interior. Safe and secure, the three companions put out their drones and relax while their Thibrans monitor the drone feeds on multiple screens.

The less-dense areas of the Amazon had been hit hard by the dinosaurs. People had fled deep into the jungle to escape and had only started to show themselves in the last few months reoccupying parts of Belem. Now the electronics have started working again, more and more survivors are trickling out of the jungle.

The drones spot a group of Adamu midway across the two-and-a-half-mile-long Sebastiao Rabelo de Olivera Bridge running for their lives with a pack of Conpex on their tails. Pulixef has a brilliant idea. He sends up a modified drone to carry it out.

A group of six native men from Mosquerio are trying to get home after hiding in the jungle for months. The dinosaurs are all dead. They had seen it with their own eyes, as the last of the Pesadelos Dinossauros had died. They were right in the middle of the bridge when a pack of Conpex smelt and saw them. They gave out one almighty roar and charged after the men. After ten minutes of hard running, it was obvious the dinosaurs would catch them.

Estevo risks a look over his shoulder while running at full speed. A slathering dinosaur is mere feet away. He closes his eyes and gives up a silent prayer for it to be quick. He had seen it too many times when it was not…The screams still haunt him at night. Behind his tightly closed eyes, he does not see the bright flash of green light.

"Martin! Estevo is starting to awaken."

"Good, Joao, we will all need our wits about us for this. Tell him not to go near the flickering green fence. We don't want anybody else getting injured." Francisco is sobbing in his cage cradling a ruined hand.

There are six of them. Estevo, Martin, Joao, Alfonso, Abel, and Francisco. They awoke lying on individual metallic pads in ten-foot square shimmering green cages. Francisco had gone over and touched the green shimmering wall of his.

In a flash of light, his fingers were gone! Just a burnt meat smell left behind. They can see through the green curtain of their cages, and not ten feet away is another set of cages containing dinosaurs. At least a dozen of the things. What's happened? Who saved their lives…And for what reason?

"Brilliant, Pulixef. Simply brilliant." The pair of hunters bow, acknowledging their friends' idea of using the Adamu to create their own 'Games' venue.

Pulixef grins saying, "I hope you both have plenty of credits because our mini Games are about to begin."

Their original energy shield had been broken down to house their captives individually, and each cage sits on top of a grav-plate. Their mini Games stadium is the remaining forty-foot section of the fence into which their fighters will be thrown.

Francisco panics as his cage elevates off the ground and moves towards the larger enclosure. It touches the other fence section and starts to blend into it. A panel in front of him shimmers red and then disappears. Francisco is now in the larger round cage. Across from him, the wall shimmers red and outbounds a dinosaur. In three strides, it's on him.

He tries to defend himself. Screaming his lungs out, he valiantly tries to push the creature's head back away from his body. The seven-foot Conpex shreds what's left of his hand and starts to tear into his arms with vicious bites. Then with a kick of its back leg, Francisco is on the ground. The Conpex holds him there with one foot as its sharp teeth tear open his stomach and start to drag out mouthfuls of intestine. It contentedly munches away at the now silent and still Francisco Desota.

The other Conpex are growling and screaming at the smell of the blood. The humans are screaming for mercy.

One after the other, they are fed to the Conpex for sport. The three Anunnaki bet between themselves to see how long it takes for the Conpex to kill and consume each Adamu.

It's great entertainment. They record it to sell to the Games pay-per-view channel. They are always looking for stuff like this.

# Ryongsong District
# Kim Jong-un's Central
# Luxury Mansion

The Koban smelt the blood as soon as they moved into the large opulent building. Deep under the building, they find torture chambers. It's the ideal location for dinner guests. They waste no time in getting some. Gigi and Lola are slowly slicing up two young people who were in the wrong place at the right time. Captured by the Kobans most brainwashed and trusted thralls within the North Korean military. These snatch teams scour the populace for just the right body type that the Koban prefer. Mid-teens, full of life, and as juicy as hell.

The teenagers are barely alive at this point. Both are lying on surgical tables while the Koban in draconian form slice off sections of flesh while they chat amicably to each other about how good they have it with the Koreans virtually worshipping them like gods and supplying them with continuous fresh food. The blood freely running down gutters on both sides of the tables supplies the pair with drinks along with their meal. They are concerned with what Anibuna will do with them now that the world is in Anunnaki's hands. They are well protected by their North Korean thralls, but what about Scarlet? She is trapped in America. All on her own.

Talk of the devil.

The long voice call from 'Scarlet' is full of fear.

"Cousins! I think Anibuna plans to kill us all. I am sure this hunt he has organised is a smoke screen to get to us. Be warned. I am fleeing for my life."

"Come to us, cousin. Together we are stronger. With our North Korean thralls to defend us, we are especially safe, and if push comes to shove with the Anunnaki, we have nuclear weapons we can use." Gigi growls out returning the long voice call.

"I don't know if I will be able to get out of the country. Can you send me transport? I can be at any airport your people can get to."

"We will send our best to bring you over, cousin. Stay safe. We will arrange it today."

Scarlet aka Joaxona sits back in her chair and smiles saying, "That went better than I could have hoped. Now where do we arrange for the pick-up to happen? It has to be away from any of our friends."

"The Andrend Poltox. Anibuna already told you to use one of their bases." Smiles Zin.

"True, Zin, he did. Which base would be best?"

"Kirtland Airforce Base. I believe their dome is on the runway next to the base."

"Okay, sisters. Let's go see the Poltox."

# Kirkland AFB

Hanger Road South-East is where the Poltox erected their dome. A shimmering green energy shield surrounds the grounded Poltox troop carrier which acts as the security forces base and staging area. A guard stands before the entrance to the shield barrier. His rifle was held by its sling across his chest.

'Ping!' the motion detector in his battle helmet sounds alert. His HUD in the battle helmet shows an incoming small craft. It is emitting a Gishma Anunnaki signal, but being a professional brood trooper, Coplonip is taking no chances. He calls it into his brood leader.

"That was a good idea, Loaxona, bringing down a skimmer from the moon base, it makes this more believable to our Poltox friends over there." Joaxona grins over to her sister. Xoanona glides the skimmer to a halt forty feet from the guard.

All three Silvenex get out of the skimmer and walk casually up to the guard. Joaxona asks politely if they can ask the brood leader for some assistance.

Coplonip had already called his superior, and brood leader Jendenip was already on his way.

Jendenip strides up to the guard who snaps to attention and deactivates the shield. The green shimmer turns red and Jendenip strides through.

"You must be Anibuna's Silvenex. We were instructed by Senior Judge Durnesson up in the ship to give you all the assistance you need in your effort to track down the last of the two hells blasted Koban. So Anibuna is doing something right in that regard at least. What is it you require, Silvenex?"

"Just the use of the airbase runway, brood leader. We need to allow an aircraft to land and take off again without triggering your defensive turrets."

"Is that all?"

"Yes, a simple thing."

"Consider it done, Silvenex. When would you require this?"

Joaxona through Scarlet's previous long voice call to the Koban knows the plane is on its way.

"Tomorrow morning, brood leader."

Jendenip gives a stiff bow, returns through the barrier, and walks back to the ship. Coplonip gives them a respectful nod and closes the barrier. It shimmers a solid green.

"Well, we now wait on our taxi, sisters. Let's do some planning. I think you two should subsume the crew. It will give us more scope to move about when we get to Korea. They are only expecting me to be there, remember."

The sisters revert to their Chinese bodies while Joaxona revives Scarlet. They dress and apply make-up. Within a short while, there stand three stunning-looking human females. Joaxona aka Scarlet will offer the crew the two Chinese females as a reward for coming to take her back to Korea.

A Gulfstream G650ER is on its final approach to Kirtland Airforce Base. They have been told to land and refuel at any airport they liked on their way over. The two-man crew, Pilot Do Hyun-Bak, and his Co-Pilot Joo Won-Cha are surprised at the access they have to American airspace. The Supreme Leader has indeed, along with the dinosaurs conquered the Americans. Pride swells in their chests as they fly over their enemy's landmass.

Wheels kiss the tarmac right on top of the large painted number twenty-six at the start of the runway. With a plume of blue smoke from the tyres, they are down. They taxi over to where three females are standing next to a refuelling bowser. They had been given a description of their contact from no other than Kang Kun-Mo himself. The Supreme Leader's deputy, which had been a great honour for them both. Do Hyun-Bak screams harshly back into the cabin for the stewardess to open the door and greet their honoured guest. She does so quickly. She has already been beaten and raped by the two men and is completely cowed by the experience. She is positive they will kill her when this trip is over.

Ha Rin-Kim, the stewardess, is surprised to see two petite Chinese women and a slightly taller Caucasian female resembling Marilyn Monroe standing at the bottom of the folding stairs she just deployed. She ushers them up the stairs and into the plush interior of the corporate jet.

The pilot and his sidekick bow to the women. Openly leering at them, they tell them to sit and relax while they refuel the jet.

As soon as they are gone, the air hostess warns them about the men's utter disregard for females. Telling them of her own beatings and rape. Joaxona asks the obviously terrified woman if she would like to stay in America and be safe from the men. She instantly agrees weeping that her family were South Koreans and had all been killed in the invasion. She has no one left. Joaxona aka Scarlet tells the woman to go into the kitchen area and close the curtain. She is to ignore anything she hears in the next few minutes, and not to come out until she comes for her.

Scarlet walks down the stairs and waves over to the two men. They stride arrogantly over to see what the gorgeous white woman wants.

"For your services to the state, the two Chinese women are for you. Use them as you see fit. Go introduce yourselves and explain to them what you require of them."

The look of degenerate lust on their faces is obscene. They virtually sprint up and into the arms of the waiting Silvenex.

Loaxona and Xoanona review the memories of the men they just subsumed and think to themselves they have done womankind a great service in terminating this pair of degenerate, web-fouled, carapace lickers.

They go up into the flight deck and start prepping the jet for take-off.

Joaxona gets the stewardess to collect all that she needs from the jet. Food, water, clothing and leads her off the plane. She sends a call to Zin via her versatile wrist shield which also houses a comms unit to explain about the Korean woman. He will send someone down in the SRC51 to pick her up. The girl weeps with relief and slowly lowers herself onto the ground as her legs turn to jelly. Joaxona tells her to wait here for someone to come and pick her up. She gives the young woman a hug and bids her farewell.

The Gulfstream streaks down the runway towards Korea, and a family reunion.

# Thera Three Spaceport
# Ponta Delgada, Azores Islands

Another family reunion is taking place. Stex has spread his little band of Boldonians throughout the planet. His main warehouse is still in Hong Kong, but he has satellite warehouses in virtually every spaceport on the planet. He moves from warehouse to warehouse to keep his sales team sharp. This month he especially wanted to be at the Azores branch for the upcoming new Games venture. His cousin Leeken had answered his call regarding the hunting venue. He is eager to see him again.

"No Discounts," cries Stex Va-D as he sees his cousin walk down the ramp of his sales transport craft. Leeken Va-D screams back, "No Discounts," in reply. Using the old Va-D motto. Both cousins give each other a big hug. Boldonians are great huggers.

"I got your message, cousin. This could be a money pit for us if it pans out." Leeken grins expectantly.

"I have already made a fortune supplying the essentials to this world, and we have it to ourselves! Locked in with my claim lodged with the trader's guild. We have it exclusively for the Va-D."

"Praise be to commerce." Both say it at the same time giving each other a wide avarice-laden grin.

"You can set up shop in my warehouse, Leeken. I will only charge you minimal rent."

"Kind of you, cousin. I will do that. What kind of minimal rent are we talking about?"

"Sixty a week, cousin."

"Forty, Stex."

"No, no, no. Fifty-five, and that's a bargain, Leeken."

"Fifty, you scoundrel."

"Okay, okay. Deal! You always were a great barterer, Leeken," Stex says with a nod of respect.

They press thumbs together and the deal is done. Stex has a couple of his sales staff carry Leeken's merchandise and gunsmithing tools into the rented section of the warehouse.

"Did I tell you young Donkx is in the shit business? He and Nilann are dredging the piles of dinosaur shit and coming up with gold, silver, platinum, and precious gems, including opals. The two of them are making themselves quite rich." Laughs Stex.

"How are they managing that?"

"It was what the Adamu were wearing at the time the dinosaurs got them. I know that look, Leeken, and I understand. I was here while it was happening remember? I did not like it. I have lived and profited off the 'Humans' as they call themselves for years. I even got to know and like some of the local Chinese traders. They are almost Boldonian in their approach to business, and as you know, business is business, and young Donkx has grasped it with both claws."

"True, true. I am not faulting your or his enterprise. I sell weapons remember, some of them are used for terrible things, but as you say business is business. So, let's do business. No Discounts."

Leeken contacts the Games channel advertising branch and has his shop broached on the Games website.

"Annnd. There you have it, Games fans. Ikell and Potts of the Holinda have just gotten themselves a massive bag of Adamu using their Silvenex to find and help bag their catch. Well done to you both. And to let you know, Games fans and competitors, famous gunsmith and supplier of prestigious arms and hunting equipment Leeken Va-D has opened shop in the Stex Va-D Azores Warehouse. More news as it happens."

Ikell and Potts often hunted together using their Black Silvenex to sniff out prey. Their hunting range is in far southern Mexico. They land in Villahermosa and set up their camp in a three-hundred-by-two-hundred-foot soccer park just off the Calle Twenty-Three Road. In front of them are the packed streets of Montes De Ame and the rest of Merida, which is on the Yucatan Peninsula. Their little group of twenty-four happy Thibrans set up two fences encompassing the entire football field and started to assemble the camp. Two Silvenex in their cages are floated out on grav-plates and positioned near the front section of their individual fence facing the densely packed buildings across the road. Two chairs and a small table are laid out with food and drink for their master's to consume. Ikell and Potts take a seat and start on the food and drink. Potts leans over to his long-time hunting and betting buddy and states, "Bet you a hundred credits, my Black finds more Adamu than your sorry excuse for a tracker."

"Make it a hundred and fifty, Potts, and you have a bet."

"On three," states Ikell.

"On three," replies Potts.

Both start to count up and on three both press the buttons that release their Silvenex from their cages. They both slink away into the streets of Montes De Ame searching for Adamu.

With the power and electronics coming back on and the dinosaurs dying off, people were coming out of hiding places and starting to put shattered lives back together.

The Silvenex run across Calle Thirty-Eight and then the two Blacks take separate routes. One runs down Calle Twenty-Seven, the other down Calle Twenty-Three A. The startled people run from these monstrous giant insects. They flee before them right into the waiting green-tinted enclosures.

The Silvenex continue this for hours. Sometimes picking up small Adamu and carrying them screaming into the cages. By the end of the day, the cages are full of weeping, crying, women and children. All the men are away hunting for food.

A quick head count of their captives declares Ikell the winner by six.

"Bet you another hundred and fifty, I can kill all mine faster than you, Potts."

"On three," states Ikell.

"On three," replies Potts.

The terrified screams of the trapped people can be heard miles away as the two intrepid hunters shoot the Adamu in their enclosures. Ikell won again. The Holinda are maybe the cruellest of the Anunnaki. These two stalwart representations of their culture back this statement up to the hilt.

The two Black Silvenex weep silently in their cages.

# Ryongsong District, Central Luxury Mansion North Korea

The driver sent by Gigi and Lola to pick up their cousin had not been told anything about the two pilots, but he knew better than to question anything that happened around the new Supreme Leaders. He has heard stories that would turn your hair grey. He is just happy to drop them off, return the car to the garage, and get out of the way. The tales of blood-curling screams coming from the basement of the large house are many. He pulls up in front of the main door and a servant comes out and smartly opens the door of the limousine. He salutes as Joaxona aka Scarlet walks out. She imperiously waves the two pilots to follow her. The servant leads the way into the house.

Gigi and Lola in their female forms do a little dance clapping their hands together and squealing in delight at the sight of their long-lost cousin. They all do a group hug then Lola asks what the pilots are doing here with her. Scarlet gives them a wicked grin and says she enjoyed their company so much on the flight over that she wants them to join them for dinner. Licking her lips at the same time.

The two sisters burst out laughing, and lead 'Scarlet' down to the 'dining room.' As soon as the two Koban enter the white-tiled torture chamber, the three Silvenex strike. Within moments, the change takes place. Reviewing the memories of the last Koban on the planet throws up a nice little surprise.

Hoeryong Concentration Camp, or Camp Twenty-Two as it is known, is hell on earth for its unfortunate inmates. Situated in the far north-east of the country, it's a desolate foreboding place. Few people who are sent there survive for long. It makes the Nazi death camps look like Disney Land.

Kang Kun-Mo and Yon Song-Choi aka Gigi and Lola had thrown a dozen or so dissident North Koreans who wanted to run the country fairly and fully merge with the south in harmony and peace, straight into the prison to shut them up. They couldn't be allowed to interfere with the food stock. The Koban liked the way they were brainwashed into thinking the leaders were almost gods. The do-gooder dissidents had started to gather quite a mass of sympathetic followers before it was brought to the Koban's attention and from there, the unlucky Koreans were sent straight to the hell, that is Camp Twenty-Two.

Do Hyun-Chay is sick and feverish. He is being treated as best they can by his two friends and fellow conspirators for a free and harmonious Korea. Joo Won-Chi and Chin Mae-Ku are all that are left of their fledgling peace movement. Do Hyun-Chay, their leader, is very near death. When the guards drag them out of the barracks and throw them in the back of a military truck, they all thought they were going to be executed.

The hospital comes as a complete surprise!

The three men are treated for their various ailments. Fed and groomed, they are then ushered into the presence of the Supreme Leaders themselves. The room is full of dignitaries, senior military officers, and a plethora of television cameras. In a fanfare of martial music, the Supreme Leaders talk to their brainwashed audience.

"People of Korea. We, your leaders, are going to consolidate our grip on America, by joining our beloved Supreme Leader Kim Jong-Un. His American advisor Miss Scarlet here brought us his message. We will leave Korea in the safe hands of Do Hyun-Chay and his deputies, Joo Won-Chi, and Chin Mae-Ku. Listen to their reforms and obey their teachings as if it were Kim Jong-Un himself who gave the command. We will be leaving immediately. Do not let us down."

A stunned trio bows and says they will make Korea a place where people will be proud to call home.

The two Supreme Leaders and their Caucasian liaison to Kim Jong-Un go out to a waiting limousine and get whisked away to the airport where they immediately reboard the waiting fuelled and warmed-up corporate jet. Assuming the form of the pilots, they head back to the USA. Once airborne, they set the autopilot and revert to their Chinese female forms and relax in the luxurious jet along with Scarlet. On landing back at the Randorian Embassy, they leave the jet parked in a nearby hangar. Moments later, the SRC51 lands and they are whisked off back to the moon base.

# Florida, USA

Lorrt and Hinpat of the Idonax Anunnaki land their skimmer in a car park beside Raymond James Stadium and set up their hunting camp. They have twenty-four Thibrans between them and a single Blue Silvenex. Their security fence is erected in the empty car park by the Thibrans. They intend to use the nearby stadium for a little fun.

The duo sets up their drones to do a search of the area. The initial flight showed a lot of Adamu present. It will be the Blues' job to flush them out. The Thibrans soon erected the barrier fence and set up viewing screens for the search drones.

The dinosaurs that tore through Florida did an enormous amount of damage and took many thousands of lives. Especially among the elderly that abounded in its many suburbs. The local hunting clubs early on fought back. Working in teams using high-calibre weapons, they had brought down many a dinosaur and most of the clubhouses had a mounted dinosaur head or two on display.

Things in Florida are coming back together since the power has come back on. Some of the roads have even been cleared to a degree of abandoned cars and trucks. Then a spaceship is seen coming down to land. The hunting club members go on high alert again. Scouts go on top of buildings to act as an early warning system. It is one of these that spots the small craft land next to Raymond James Stadium.

"Tully, tell Bill that the ship we saw circling the city has landed, and about two dozen little grey men are building a fence around the carpark next to Raymond James Stadium. We need more people out here."

"Okay Wilks, we will send as many as we can get. You stay safe now. Ya-Hear."

"Sure, Tully. I will keep reporting what they are doing."

David Wilks makes himself as comfortable as he can. Next to him is his cousin Orville. He turns to his cousin and drawls, "Well, Duffus, you may get a chance to fire that old Sharps Fifty-Cal, after all. How many rounds you got for that thing anyway?"

"Thirty, Davey boy. All loaded my own self."

Orville had inherited the Sharps from their grandfather and had named the rifle after him. It was an old 1874 Sharps 50–70 Buffalo rifle, and Orville was deadly with the thing on the club's firing range.

Lorrt and Hinpat get the Thibrans to glide out of the Silvenexians; cage. They will have to look for another Blue. This one is so broken; it barely performs unless shocked repeatedly. Several little jabs of the collar's activation stud get the mentally destroyed Silvenex to shuffle out of the cage and stagger through the red-tinted shield gate section. Han-Ib-Oca stands with her back to the energy fence wishing with all her heart that her misery will someday end.

"Jesus! Orville, look at this thing. It's a big fucking insect."

Orville looks over with the binoculars and if this isn't a good enough target to check out the Sharps with, he doesn't know what would be.

"It's in range, cousin. I am going to see if I can get it with 'old Gramps'."

Orville thumbs back the hammer and settles behind the rifle. Looking through the peep sight, he lines it up with the centre mass of the creature standing in front of the opaque green wall. The boom of the rifle is deafening. The smoke from the black powder cartridge temporarily obscures the target from sight.

The fifty-calibre bullet tears her left arm off almost making Han-Ib-Oca's wish a reality. She lies there hoping she will bleed out. The Anunnaki's heads snap up at the sound of the rifle. They see their Blue slump to the ground with a huge amount of pale orange blood pooling under its missing arm. They both look at each other and grin. They have found a real challenge and the Blue had been insured anyway, so win-win. They order some of the Thibrans to deal with the wounded Silvenex.

"Great shot, man, you nailed that sucker good," Wilks cries excitedly.

Orville pushes down on the trigger guard and the breach spits out the empty cartridge. He slides in a new round and closes the breach.

"Thanks, man. This is a great rifle."

Using the HUDs on their battle helmets, the Anunnaki calculate the trajectory of the shot that had wounded their Blue. They pick up their point-four rifles and stride out to stand beside their fallen hunting dog. The Thibrans stop the bleeding and cauterise the stump. Han-Ib-Oca whimpers in pain.

"Look at this shit, cousin! Birdmen, and they have weapons. Shoot quick, Davey."

The pair shoot at the Anunnaki. Both shots hit true, and both shots get absorbed by Anunnaki's point-four shields.

The Anunnaki casually aim and shoot back. Their shots blow holes straight through the men spraying the back wall of the roof crimson.

The Anunnaki then stride over to their kills and remove the heads for trophies.

"Annnd. There you have it. Games Fans. Our first hunting dog is out of the running. All winning betters on this should put your ticket into your nearest Games betting outlet to collect your winnings. Any hunting dog suppliers out there? Lorrt and Hinpat are probably going to be looking for a replacement. The games procurement division can always supply quality merchandise as well, so please contact your nearest Games outlet for details. More action as it happens, Game fans, stay tuned."

# Eden Base Control Room

The friends sit staring at the screen as the Games news channel gives out the latest on Anibuna's Safari Experience.

"We need to do something about this shit, Boss. They are hunting people for entertainment, for fucks sake," growls Norman Vincenti.

"Oh, we will, Norman, we will." Looking over to Willie and Jake, Zin asks, "How are your anti-sniper skills, guys?"

"Out-fucking-standing." Both say at the same time and grin at each other with evil smiles.

"Remember, Ramadi buddy."

"Yep, Willie, we got that motherfucker right enough."

# Ramadi Iraq
# 2004

The Private awoke that morning with an overpowering feeling of dread. For the last two days of this 'IO' (Information Operation), he had been handing out candy bars to kids and smiling for the camera crews showing how the Marines were doing their bit to capture the hearts and minds of the local populace. This morning felt different. He could barely eat any breakfast and had already puked in the head before climbing into the Humvee. The twenty-minute ride down the route Michigan to their drop-off point just east of Easy Street in downtown Ar Ramadi is uneventful, but he still cannot shake the feeling.

Nasim Al-Malik finishes his prayers, Picks up his sniper's rifle and makes his way into Ramadi. His prayers were to have the strength to kill as many of the hated infidels as he could, and if he perished doing God's work, then he went straight to Allah's Garden where he hoped to meet up with his family; all killed in a drone strike several months ago.

The Private still can't shake the bad feeling he has, but at least he gets a little kick out of seeing the kids' faces light up when he hands them a candy bar. His own little sister is the same age as most of these kids. He is just straightening up from giving a candy bar to a little girl wearing a Dora the Explorer T-shirt when a 7.62mm round went clean through his skull dropping him to the ground in a boneless heap. A scream of 'sniper' rings across the little courtyard the four Marines are in, handing out treats to the local kids. There is no cover at all. Nowhere for them to go. Nasim Al-Malik calmly and systematically kills all four of the Marines. The kids ransack their bodies for more candy.

"Willie, go find your cuddle buddy and report to Colonel Trent," Gunnery Sargent Villa grunts out.

"Hup! Gunnery Sargent." Willie races out of the tent and goes to track down Sergeant Jake Lincon, his sniper partner.

Ten minutes later, the pair are at attention in front of their CO, Colonel Trent.

"Okay, men, at ease. We have a situation. There's an Iraqi sniper out there that's already killed four Marines and wounded six more. I want this fucker dead before any more good Marines get taken out by this bastard." He looks the pair straight in the eye and says, "I know you are the guys for the job. You will have the full support of the Marines in the area. He is working in the downtown district just off Easy Street. Go get this son of a bitch."

Both men smartly salute. About face, then leave the tent.

"Do you know any of the guys this shit heel tagged, Willie?"

"Nope, Jake, but that doesn't matter. Their brothers and we get to find the bastard and punch his ticket for them."

"Go rustle up a Hummer and I will put our kit together."

"Okay, Jake, see you in a few." Willie runs over to the motor pool to requisition a vehicle and driver. The hunt is on.

The Americans are getting smarter. It's been hours since he's glimpsed a target. The last one only showed a leg. His shot shattered the knee. Nearly severing the limb. The cries of the young Marine calling for his mother were music to his ears. He managed to record it on his phone. When he could, he would try and photograph his kills. He is amassing quite a collection.

Al-Malik sets up his sniper's hide in the basement of a partly bombed-out building. An air vent gives him a great view of a crossroads two hundred yards away, plus he has an easy escape route using a tunnel into an adjacent building. He calmly waits for targets, slipping prayer beads through his fingers to pass the time.

Willie and Jake are given the call sign of mongoose and attach themselves to a roving patrol of eight Marines. They parked the Humvees just short of a crossroads and started to make their way in on foot. The squad's point man should put money on the next lottery. Because he is one lucky SOB.

Al-Malik sees the point man late. He was distracted by a scorpion that had crawled onto his arm. By the time he killed it, the point man was nearly past his position. A hasty move of his rifle re-acquires the target. His bullet slams into the soldier's helmet, goes straight through and out the other end without hitting his head. The impact knocks him onto his side. The other men dive for cover screaming 'Sniper!'

Willie and Jake start their hunt. They know roughly where the shot came from, but any decent sniper would have relocated after taking the shot. The two-man sniper team go high and get up onto a roof with good coverage of the surrounding area. Willie radios into the sergeant of the squad they're with, call sign 'Snake Charmer'.

"Snake Charmer, Mongoose. Try and flush the bastard out sarge so we can get a bead on him."

"Mongoose, Snake Charmer, we are going to start house to hou…" Another shot cracks out. "Bastard just got Taylor." The inside window of one of the Humvees is splashed red as the driver's head explodes from the impact of Al-Malik's 7.62mm bullet.

"We have an idea now, Snake Charmer. He's low, two buildings over next to that chemist's shop."

"Go get the son of a bitch, Mongoose."

Both men race down from the roof and run down the street to a bomb-damaged bus that is lying on its side. They crawl into the bus and start to scope the buildings in front of them. The sun is now very low at their backs casting long shadows across the street. Willie and Jake set up their night vision gear.

Al-Malik grins. It's getting dark. Soon, it will be safe to exit the building and return to the basement where he has been spending his nights. He even got a good photo of the dead soldier in the vehicle. Praise be to Allah.

The Marines are pissed at losing another brother Marine and start doing vigorous house-to-house searches to try and find the elusive sniper.

Willie and Jake scan the lower levels of each building. The night vision gear makes everything a green-tinted version of daylight.

Nasim Al-Malik is in complete darkness. His blackened face and dark loose clothing make him totally invisible to the naked eye, but not to the state-of-the-art AN/PVS-26 night vision scope fitted to Jake's M24 or Willie's night vision spotter's scope. Jake's shot takes Al-Malik in his throat blowing out a sizeable chunk of his spine as it exited the back of his neck, ending the reign of terror he had inflicted on the Marines in Iraq in 2004.

# Games Sports Channel
# Present Day

"Annnd. There you have it, Games fans. We have a rogue hunter in play. This has not happened for quite some time." Consulting his notes, he looks back seriously into the camera. "Ginumm of the Hitori used a hunt to eliminate three of his clan rivals in the Hitori hierarchy. This is totally against the rules, of course. Unless the rogue hunter backdates his entry and pays the appropriate late fees to the Games administration department within three days of the incident. Coli and Linn of the Holinda where both shot in the head and killed this morning in their hunting preserve in Southern India. Linn had been skinned. Something we have not seen since the 'Yonath Troubles' when they used to skin rivals and display the skins for all to see. So, this may be a rogue Yonath who doesn't like the fact that someone is resurrecting a different version of their Games."

"Their pair of Black Silvenex were also taken. Again, any hunter would not pass up free Silvenex. So, it's no surprise they are gone. Nothing has been seen of their Thibran servants, but they may have just run away. Graphic footage of this can be sourced on our pay-per-view channel five. More on this as it unfolds, Games fans. Betting values on this are extremely high. So, any lucky winners, send in your tickets and collect your winnings. Keep tuned, Game fans, for further news."

**Tamil Nadu. Southern India.**

Coli and Linn have received information from the hunting society that their area is teaming with game, and to make things interesting for the pair of respected hunters, sixty Conpex have been released as well.

The experienced hunters land in a large open space just off Madurai Road in Rameswaram next to the Hotel Amman Residency. Their ever-efficient Thibrans quickly set up their camp and established their security enclosure. Their Black Silvenex are brought out ready to go hunt out the elusive prey.

India had been hit hard by the Koban dinosaurs. Millions had been killed. Fortunately, nearby Sri Lanka never got any. So, a lot of Indians fled to Sri Lanka for safety. With the dinosaurs dying off and the return of modern electronics, the Indians started to return from the island and reoccupied the peninsula leading inland from nearby Sri Lanka. To their horror, a spaceship lands in the area, and if that's not bad enough, dinosaurs have returned. Mass panic ensues as the Conpex chase down humans and feast.

The alien bird men, at first, are seen as saviours, as they systematically kill the dinosaurs, removing their heads and stacking them in neat piles next to their green-tinted enclosure. Relief turns to horror when two local men approach the aliens to thank them for their intervention with the dinosaurs. The Holinda cruelly laugh as two human heads join the pile. The rest of the humans, on seeing that barbaric act, flee in panic.

Willie and Jake had been shuttled down from the moon to meet up with Joaxona and her sisters who had just arrived back from Korea. Using the SRC51 that Clive Miles-Smythe brought down will give them the ability to bounce about the planet unseen. Clive goes back up to Eden Base with an Anunnaki shuttle that had dropped off supplies for Doplon's Base on Earth.

Jake, Willie and the three Blues take off and head for the coordinates of the hunters in Southern India and touch down unseen in the SRC51, two miles away from the Anunnaki's enclosure. They then conduct a hasty search for a suitable sniper's perch. They find the ideal spot, on top of the Rameswaram Hotel situated just next to the railway station. The four-storey hotel is one of the tallest buildings in the area. It's a mile and a half away from the Anunnaki's green-tinted enclosure giving them the ideal viewpoint to scope out their targets. With the full team being equipped with the modified spotter glasses, the Anunnaki's compound is shown in stark relief. What they see is two caged Black Silvenex being tormented by a little group of vicious Thibrans poking them with pieces of sharpened wire.

"Look at this shit! How good do you think their shields will be, Joaxona?"

"Unknown, Willie. They can be anything up to a point-eight. Ours are only point fours remember."

"Look one of them just handed that Thibran his brag-bag while he's checking out something from that pile of…oh! Fuck, it's a human head. Christ, that's gross, but that's our ticket to hitting these sonsofbitches. Once that bag leaves their hand their shield is gone. Can you get a bead on this bastard while he is…"

Hum! Jake's rifle cuts out his last words.

"Out-fuckin-standing, Jake. That was a real quick draw."

Downrange Coli loses one side of his head, as the point-four hard-light slug tears through his left eye and blows the back of his head off in a spray of orange blood.

Linn's reactions are swift. Using the reverse trajectory function in his helmet, he immediately fires back along the same line as the incoming rounds. He sprays the area with his rifle on fully automatic. The point-three pulses get absorbed by the sniper's shields. They immediately relocate.

Linn cannot see the results of his fire. So, he retreats behind the shield wall and sends out both Silvenex to deal with the unknown sniper.

The Silvenex race towards the hotel; their shock collars lash them to greater speeds, not knowing they will be running into three Blues.

The Blacks are trapped and webbed by the three Blues as soon as they enter the building. Willie uses his handgun and carefully blows the crystals from the Silvenexian's throats. They immediately stop struggling. Their six eyes are looking everywhere at once in panic. Then they settle on Joaxona. Green drool slides down their mandibles and they twitch slightly as if expecting a lash from their shock collars. Joaxona shakes her head. The poor Blacks may be beyond help.

Willie and Jake have relocated to a different part of the hotel and keep the dome under surveillance.

Below them, the captured Blacks start to buck and scream in the webbing net. Their minds have finally snapped in their brief time of freedom from the collar.

Joaxona whispers to her sisters and then stands back bowing her head. Loaxona and Xoanona assimilate the tortured Blacks and the room goes still. Joaxona then frees her sisters from the web.

Both sisters stand trembling with tears streaming down their faces as they review their tortured host's memories. Some of the things the Holinda did to them were horrendous. The surviving Anunnaki will suffer. Oh! He will suffer for a long, long time once the two new Blacks get a hold of him.

Joaxona is covered in a light web and slung between the two assimilated Blacks. They walk back to the green-walled enclosure. Ferness calls out, "Master! We killed the Anunnaki sniper and captured his Silvenex."

Sunessde aka Xoanona holds up Willie's point-three rifle and calls out, "Here is his weapon, master."

An astonished Linn drops the shield and ushers in the Silvenex. Joaxona is dropped at his feet. Several of his Thibrans crowd around to see their master's success. Glorying vicariously with him in his victory.

"Give me the rifle, Silvenex." Without even looking around, he hands his brag-bag to his nearest fawning Thibran servant. As soon as it leaves his hands, all three Silvenex strike. The webbing that covered Joaxona was just for show. It has no stickiness or strength in it. It tears like tissue paper as Joaxona springs up from the ground. She and Loaxona hammer Linn into unconsciousness. Then disgustedly throw him into one of the Silvenexian's cages. Yellow feathers lie on the ground where they are torn from his head and wings as he is thrown into the cage.

Xoanona shoots the Thibrans with the rifle set on fully automatic. These little devils used to torture the Black Silvenex in their cages mercilessly. Mimicking their sadistic Holinda masters.

She walks around the entire perimeter making sure every one of the little web-rotted slime grubs is dead.

Willie and Jake had covered the sisters all the way to the enclosure with the Super Barrett. They race across the railway tracks to join them. As they run into the enclosure, they see a battered Anunnaki in a cage with three seriously pissed-off Silvenex just standing there staring at a very, very, frightened Linn.

Joaxona looks over her shoulder at the snipers and asks in a cold, hard voice they have never heard before if they would please leave them for a little while. They have some Silvenexian-only business to conduct with the Anunnaki.

They nod their heads in reply. Willie picks up his rifle and the two Anunnaki brag-bags then they walk out of the enclosure. A long-drawn-out scream sends shivers up the battle-hardened Marines' spines. Willie starts to look back, just as a white-as-a-sheet Jake looks quickly back to his front after glimpsing what was happening back in the compound.

"D-don't look, Willie man. J-just, just don't look." Shudders Jake.

The screams behind them rise in pitch. Then when you think that's the worst, the next drawn-out scream tops even that. The Marines walk faster back to the stealth ship. Jake hoping to hell he can get rid of the image of the Blues starting to skin the Anunnaki alive from his memory.

Back on the ship, Willie contacts Zin to relate how the mission went. He tells Zin they have two brag-bags to check out, and asks if Zin have any more targets for them to hunt down.

Several hours later, in walk three gore-covered Silvenex. Without a word to the humans, they head for the showers.

Back in their Chinese female forms, the Silvenex meet up with Willie and Jake in the recreation area. The trio are all smiles and bubbly as if nothing had happened mere hours ago.

Willie asks them if everything is all right. The Silvenex give them such a look of pure friendship and love it takes them by surprise.

"Yes, we are fine, and we got the chance to free two of our cousins from a fate worse than death. They can now live forever within Xoanona and Loaxona." Both give big smiles at the mention of their names. "Now, what is our next target? Ideally, we need to get your rifle upgraded, and I just found out that Leeken is here."

"Now that would be a good thing, and what's the chance we can get our shields done at the same time." Grins Jake.

"We can only ask."

Zin is contacted to see if he can get to Leeken without tipping their hand to the Anunnaki, or the Poltox Peacekeeping Force. It is decided that Tonvik, Joadin's second-in-command aka Zin will pay the gunsmith a visit after Zin has a word to him first of course.

"Hello, Leeken, is it safe to talk?"

"Zin! I had not thought I would hear from you for quite a while. How is your feisty human female?"

"She is still shooting straight."

"Haha, very good, Zin, very good. Now how can I help you?"

Zin tells him of the blockade and the fact the Anunnaki are killing humans in the hunts. He wants to make sure his friends are protected. So, he asks if he can supply upgraded shields and if can he modify a rifle to be more powerful than point-five. Ideally, he wants something that will beat a point-eight shield. Leeken asks Zin to come down to the shop. He has a couple of ideas that might work. At a cost, of course. Zin chuckles to himself…Typical Boldonian. Zin arranges the meeting for the following morning. Reverting to the Anunnaki form of Tonvik, he heads to Eden's hanger bay.

"Tonvik to Belatan ship. Requesting passage down to Thera Three. I have some business on the planet."

"Permission granted, Anunnaki. Enter the atmosphere at your discretion."

Zin takes a small shuttle down and lands beside the Boldonian Warehouse. Picking up the gear he wants modified, he puts it on a grav-cart and walks up to the door giving the pass phrase he and Leeken had worked out so that Leeken will know the Anunnaki at his shop door is really Zin.

"No Discounts," cries Zin, aka Tonvik.

"No Discounts," replies Leeken. "Come in, come in. What do you require, Zin? Or do I call you by the Anunnaki's name?"

"No, Zin's fine. Is your door locked?"

"Yes, I only ever have one customer at a time, for security's sake. Now what do you need, Zin?."

Zin brings out Jake's Super Barrett and hands it to Leeken.

Leeken's mouth twists in disgust. "You did this with a replicator, didn't you?"

"Yes."

"They are okay, but it's never quite right. So, this is a point-four converted pulse rifle. I can easily change the barrel and bring it up to point-five, but you want more than that. A chance encounter with a truly evil scale tick recently got me tinkering with Tiban crystals."

"Woah, that's what they use in space weaponry. The big sixes and eights that you get on battleships and cruisers have them. My own 117 has sixes."

"Well, I found a way of using small shards of Tiban crystal that I can fit into a rifle barrel. Lunderon had a roughly cut piece on top of a walking stick which will give off a tremendous pulse of maybe point-eight or nine. My cut and shaped crystals are much smaller but focus the reaction better. On testing, I was getting one point two."

"That's unbelievable. Can you convert Jake's rifle?"

"Yes, no problem, but it will cost you. What do you have for me? You hinted at more antique weapons." Leeken is rubbing his hands together in anticipation.

Drawing a package from the grav-cart, Zin says, "This is a sample. These are all from this planet's last major conflict. It was called World War Two." Zin draws out an M1 Carbine fitted with a buttstock double magazine pouch, sling, and bayonet. Next, he lifts out a leather full-flap holster containing a Colt. 45 on a web belt with another double magazine holder attached. Leeken's eyes go big. He picks up the rifle and expertly examines it.

"Is this material wood? So rare other than here. It is beautifully crafted." He runs his hands along the woodwork of the rifle. Using the glasses on his head which have an X-ray function, he looks at the inner workings of the carbine. "Ah, it uses the explosive gases to prime the weapon for a new projectile, quite clever." He repeatedly operates the slide and ejects the ammunition. Then releasing the magazine, he refills it with the fifteen small bullets and reinserts it into its slot. "Splendid, Zin, simply splendid."

"I can get you two hundred of each. Plus, one thousand rounds of ammunition for both weapons. Do we have a deal? Plus, the upgraded wrist shields, of course."

Leeken holds out his thumb…"Deal."

# Leeken's Gunsmithing Workshop

Leeken quickly strips down Jake's rifle and discards the barrel removing the positive static charge unit (PSCU) mounted cleverly to look like the muzzle break. He then goes to a wall-safe and brings out a metal container. He opens it to reveal dark blue crystal shards inside. They glow with a faint pulsing light.

"I have blank barrels that will fit the rifle. It will take me a little while to fit and align the crystals. Watch if you like."

"I would love to, this is amazing."

Leeken digs out a variety of tools and gauges and then starts to work. On his forehead is a sophisticated set of goggles that let him look at the Tiban crystals as if under an electron microscope as he aligns them and inserts them into the barrel. Two hours of fascinating intricate work sees the barrel complete and the PSCU refitted. The barrel is quickly re-joined to the rifle. They both walk through to the gun range. Leeken sets up a meter next to the target that will tell them the strength of the hard-light pulse. He charges the rifle and lines up on a standard target.

'Wooom'…The noise from the rifle is totally different. Not loud, but it makes your scales tingle…The target is gone. The meter reads one point four.

Leeken looks at the meter in amazement saying, "Well, well, well. I did not expect it to be so high."

"One! One point four. Leeken, that's unbelievable. Ground artillery is one point six! You have outdone yourself, Gunsmith, that's for sure. I will add in some more old equipment as a bonus." Zin is grinning like an idiot. "What about shields?" Zin walks over to Leeken removing his wrist shield.

"Point-eight is as much as a personal shield can handle. I have heard talk of power one shields, but it's just hearsay. I can alter all of your shields to point-eight. Do you have them here?"

"Yep, they're on the cart, and here's mine." Zin hands Leeken his shield.

"Give them over here then, and I can get started."

Zin brings the wrist shields out of the cart and Leeken gets to work.

"If you are going after that scale tick, Lunderon, let me know, and I will tell you a little secret." Leeken's smile is one of pure evil.

"Annnd. There you have it, Games fans." Sparyten's trademark grin of a wide-open beak flashes onto screens everywhere the hunt is being watched. "Our rogue hunter has struck again. The betting on this individual has skyrocketed so get your bets in quick. Inipan of the Anisol. Lunderon's protégé was shot in the head. Well, we think it was a shot. Our ballistics team's quite stunned as to what may have killed the unfortunate novice hunter. Lunderon has asked permission from the Hunt Committee to be able to track down the rogue hunter himself. We will let you know the decision when it comes in. Until then stay tuned for more as it happens, Game fans."

# Inipan of the Anisol

Inipan's hunting reserve is listed as quadrant one in Europe. From his information pack, he reads that a considerable number of Adamu are in a coastal area listed as Holland. He has never seen so much water as in this place. It's unbelievable. As he circles above a large city, listed as Amsterdam, his scanners detect Adamu on the ground. Several shoot at his craft. Excellent, he will be up against armed Adamu. He is desperate to show his Uncle Lunderon that he warrants the title of top student from his hunting school.

Selecting a landing site not too far away from the Adamu, he brings the craft down to land in a park surrounded by waterways. His Thibrans immediately secure the area with an energy fence. Inipan leaves them to it. He needs bait. Studying the scanner data, there are definitely Adamu nearby. Calling over his Thibrans, he selects two to serve him lunch. The others he arms with HIS4 stun guns. They look lovingly at their young master, awaiting his orders.

"Okay, I need bait. The smaller, the better. Go into the dwellings past the watercourse and find some. I want to be laying out bait before nightfall."

Ten little bodies scream out, "We won't let you down, master."

"You had better not," growls the arrogant young hunter in reply.

The Thibrans scurry away eager to impress their young master. Lenil, the leader of this little group exhorts his fellows saying, "Let's go. The master is relying on us to find bait. We will split up and search the dwellings over there. Shout out if you find anything."

They cry out, "For Inipan." They rush towards the buildings.

A crying child is heard by Clanda and his fellow slave Raslin. They creep towards a three-storey building. The cries are getting louder. Raslin draws out his stunner and whispers to Clanda saying, "Go, get the others."

Within moments, all ten are by the door leading into the building. Lenil looks hard at his fellow slaves and then growls out, "For Inipan." And pushes the door open. The Thibrans rush into the building screaming. A startled human female looks up just as the Thibrans enter the room. She instinctively tries to protect her little charge of five babies. The oldest is nine months. She barely rises from her seat before she is shot several times by the Thibrans HIS4s.

The triumphant Thibrans load their booty onto a grav-plate and walk back to the park. The crying child is now quietly gurgling away with the other five babies.

Inipan just grunts at the Thibrans' return saying, "Freeze them." He lets the Thibrans complete their work. He is studying the layout of the park. It has an open grassy centre which is surrounded by trees. He has a hide scoped out. The grassy area is the perfect killing ground. Looking around, he points to a Thibran, it just happens to be Clanda. Inipan does not know that. He does not know or care what the slaves are called. "You! Go, revive a bait. Stake it out in the middle of the field."

Clanda rushes away to complete his master's wishes.

A child is revived. Clanda has no empathy for this thing at all. He lifts it by a leg and walks quickly into the middle of the field. The baby is screaming its lungs out. Using some twine, Clanda ties it to a metal rod he drives into the ground. The little Adamu is flat on its back kicking and waving its arms. The noise from the thing is hurting his ears. He's more than delighted to be away from it.

A Conpex prowling on the opposite side of the park hears the squealing child. It is drawn to the sound of obvious prey. It can smell the prey now. Slowly, it inches forward. All of its senses alert for danger. There in front of it is the prey. One final sniff of the air and a look around convinces the large predator that it is safe. It bounds forward grabbing the baby in its mouth. It keeps going until it is in the trees at the other end of the park some thirty feet away where it settles down to consume its meal.

Arrg! His uncle would have had him flogged. He was distracted fiddling with his brag-bag when a Conpex took the bait neat as you please. He turns to one of his Thibrans and orders it to revive another bait and tie it to the stake. The Conpex may come back for another one. He could always say he was throwing bait to attract a kill. Yes, that would work. Pride restored, he watches the Thibran tie a wriggling little Adamu to the stake with a length of twine. Inipan settles behind his rifle watching the bait wriggle. He, like any hunter anywhere, has no interest in the welfare of his bait. None at all.

In the nearby trees just out of sight, the Conpex is finishing off the tender flesh of its easy meal. The tantalising smell of more meat is in the air.

On the same side of the park, a patrol of three Dutchmen from the Korps Commandotroepen hears a baby crying. Curious, they walk towards the noise. Night is approaching casting long shadows throughout the dense foliage. Gripping their HK416 assault rifles tighter, they move through the park. Squad leader Hendrik Claasen steps on the feasting Conpex. It jumps up with a hissing growl, slashing out with claws and teeth. The soldiers' ballistic body armour and helmets stop any major injuries. Half a magazine at point-blank range from Corporal Aldert DeVrie's rifle through its head stops the eight-foot reptile from doing any more damage.

Six hundred feet away, Inipan's head jerks up at the sound of the gunfire. He quickly launches a drone. Within minutes, it is sending back high-definition views of three Adamu soldiers crouched over a dead Conpex.

Inipan's beak opens wide in a grin. Now this will be one for his brag-bag. He enters the trees to his right. With the river covering his right flank, he starts to stalk the soldiers. Passing a bridge, he moves further into the trees. The soldiers are now two hundred feet in front of him, crouched on the grass still looking at the Conpex.

Seargent Claasen claps his corporal on the shoulder saying, "Well done, Aldert. We will need to tell headquarters that the neuken dinosaurs are not all dead after all. Right, let's go see where the crying is coming from."

Inipan takes aim with his sophisticated point-four rifle. The sight glows as he locks on each individual target. Ceramic plates and Kevlar armour are no defence against hard light. All three troopers get their chests blown open. With a satisfied grin, he walks forward to claim his trophies. Since these Adamu are armed, he copies his uncle, taking their trigger fingers and weapons as trophies.

Zin's sniper team have no real plan. They will tackle any hunter they come across. The nearest is in Holland. He will do. Joaxona flies in from Jan Mayen Island. It only takes twenty minutes. Scans on the way in show where the Anunnaki's craft is sitting in trees behind a sixty-foot-wide circular park. On the way down, they see a human baby lying in the middle of it. It is naked and tied to a stake by one of its legs. This scaletick is using human hatchlings as bait. Joaxona lands in the trees opposite the hatchling. Xoanona quickly runs down the gangplank and frees the human infant. It is pleasantly warm against her hard body shell. Is this the only one? Or does the webworm have more? Xoanona fears there will be more.

The triple hum of Anunnaki's rifle firing at the soldiers answers the question Joaxona was about to ask Xoanona. Where had the web-snarled Anunnaki gone? They can see his Thibrans but not the hunter.

The SRC51 sits in the trees at the bottom left-hand corner of the circular park. Willie and Jake are lying on top of the ship. Jake is desperate to try out his new rifle on the motherfucker that set up a baby as bait. Willie whispers saying, "Look, Jake. The bastards just cleared the tree line. Take your shot."

Inipan walks arrogantly across the middle of the circular park. He can already see the bait is gone. He half expected as much when he went after the Adamu. He is in the middle of the circle when Jake's rifle gives out its distinctive Wooom. Inipan's head disappears in a puff of orange blood. He stands there headless for a second or two. Then slumps bonelessly to the ground. Loaxona kills the milling confused Thibrans bar one. It is trembling before her scissoring mandibles.

"Take us to the Anunnaki's ship and I will not kill you," promises Loaxona.

"Promise," pleads Raslin in a whiney voice full of sobs.

"You have my word, Thibran. I will not kill you."

"Okay, follow me." The little voice is full of hope.

Raslin takes the three Silvenex over the bridge and back to the Anunnaki hunter's shuttle. Inside are three hatchlings and an adult female, alive but in stasis. Loaxona stares hard at the quaking Thibran; her fears are confirmed.

Joaxona drags the Thibran outside and slits his throat. Well, Loaxona had promised that she would not kill him. The web mould deserved nothing less.

Willie and Jake walk over to their kill and examine the damage. "Look at this man. There's nothing left of the head. A body shot with this puppy." Lifting the rifle up. "Would probably cut you in two. You got the feather, Willie boy."

"Here, Jake." Willie hands over a white feather. Jake sticks it in the harness covering the dead Anunnaki's torso.

"Ole Carlos would be proud, Willie."

"That's for sure, man. Maybe we should paint white feathers on our combat helmets."

"Good idea, buddy. Yeah, let's do that."

What Carlos Hathcock could have done with Jake's rifle boggles the imagination.

They go to find the dead Anunnaki's brag-bag; it is lying a few feet away covered in orange blood droplets. They wipe it on the grass and walk back to the SRC51.

They can hear the squeals and gurgles of the children before they go up the ramp. The Silvenex are back in their Chinese female forms. They get directions from the woman to a local militia unit that is distributing food. Using the radio, they call ahead warning the militia of their approach. They are waiting on them as they land. The children are carried into the militia building where a great fuss is made over them. Willie and Jake get a crate of Dutch beer from the militia unit as thanks, and everyone parts in good humour wishing each other well and for the return of a free Earth.

The stealth craft returns to the safety of the frozen Arctic Circle and monitors the Games channel in order to be able to plan out their next hit on the hunters. There is only one day left in the five-day scheduled event.

Lunderon gets permission from the hunters' society to track and kill or capture the rogue hunter. Word of this gets to the Games news studios.

"Annnd. There you have it, Games fans. It's official. Lunderon of the Anisol is to track down and kill or capture the rogue hunter. The betting on this is already fierce, gentle beings, so get in quick for the best odds. More news as it happens, stay tuned, Game fans."

Willie gets some news from Zin. Leeken has been told to expect several of the hunters to come in later that day for last-minute supplies and some minor gunsmithing. They will be landing in the Azores Spaceport in three hours. What kind of damage could Jake do to a lightweight transport shuttle with the modified Super Barrett? Zin can't wait to find out.

Lunderon is at the bottom of the ramp ready to board the shuttle back to the Azores Spaceport on Porta Delgada when Cumlox of the Gishma sneers at him saying his vaunted hunter's school can't be that good if he lost his star pupil. His cronies, all Gishma laugh. While Lunderon is pondering a suitable retort, Ofintin of the Padenon slips past him and grabs the last seat.

Lunderon is furious. He has to quickly step back as the ramp starts to rise. Snarling out a curse, he turns on his heel and storms away. An unlucky Thibran walks across his path. The anger-filled strike with his walking stick kills the poor thing. It's dead before it hits the ground. It lies bleeding at the side of the path. Lunderon strides away without even a backward glance. Fifty thousand feet above him, the Gishma and the sole surviving Padenon are laughing at Lunderon's expense. Many miles in front of them, the SRC51 lands in an enclosed compound within an oil storage facility on the Azores Spaceport perimeter. The massive white tanks holding oil and fuel are right on the flight path less than a mile from the Joao Paulo II Airport which has been converted to be the Spaceport in Ponta Delgada.

Willie and Jake run down the ramp of the landed SRC51 and disappear into the night. They climb up to the top of one of the white storage tanks using the access ladders affixed to the sides of it. Once in place, they hook up a quick escape zip line. The zip line goes back down to the open rear ramp of the SRC51. The Silvenex guard the ship and watch the sniper's backs.

Willie's glasses spot the incoming transport several miles out over the sea, descending towards the spaceport. He paints the target. It glows golden in Jake's gunsight.

At two miles out and at an altitude of one thousand feet, Jake squeezes the trigger. The distinctive 'Wooom' of the weapon makes your teeth tingle. Downrange the shuttle disintegrates as the heavy light pulse tears through the body and explodes the engine's fuel cell.

The transport shuttle falls into the Atlantic sinking to the bottom in tiny pieces. Willie and Jake police up their area leaving a white feather as a calling card. They then slide down the zip line and walk into the back of the SRC51. Within two minutes, they're gone.

"Annnd. There you have it, Games fans. In a tragic accident, six of the Games' finest have been lost as their transport blew up on approach to the Azores Spaceport. Foul play cannot be ruled out, but at this time, it looks like a tragic accident. The odds on this are staggering, so any lucky ticket holder contact the Games betting hotline and collect your winnings. Stay tuned, Games fans, for more as it happens."

The Games security section investigated the crash viewing all the data and talking to witnesses. As usual, the nosey gossiping, bragging, Thibrans are their best source of information. Several Thibrans were waiting on the shuttle landing to greet their Gishma masters. The Thibrans stated they heard a weird whooshing noise just before the transport blew up. They had no idea what that was.

Radar at the airport plotted the shuttle on its approach. There was no other air traffic, and no missile launch was detected. The Games investigators put drones into the water looking for the black boxes. Later that day, they are found.

The black boxes showed no problems at all with the transport. The engine did not malfunction. The transport was struck with something travelling at speeds only matched by a meteorite or military-grade spaceship gunnery, and there were no ships in orbit. The official verdict is that the transport had been struck by a meteorite. One lucky punter who had put a single credit on that very outcome became a millionaire overnight. The Anunnaki will bet on anything.

## SRC51's Temporary Base. Jan Mayen Island. Arctic Circle.

The hit squad are having a celebration. Six! They got six of the foul creatures in one hit. On the viewscreen in the SRC51, Zin and the rest of the team on the moon call out their praise for a successful campaign so far.

"Last day, guys. How's the Wooggi holding up?" Zin grins at the screen.

"That stuff's great. Willie 'n me's had four cups of it and are as alert as we were on day one."

"Have another cup or two. The other guys said it lasted five days and then they crashed. So, don't take any chances this being day five."

"Willie, bring the flask of Wooggi. We will finish it off. We got a big day in front of us."

They both look into the comms unit's camera and toast the crew on the moon with the Wooggi.

"Death to the Anunnaki."

The same chant comes over the speakers. Time to finish this, and Jake has an idea.

When Leeken had done the conversion of the Super Barrett, Jake had asked Zin to get the old barrel, which was easily changeable. Jake wanted the option of precision at both spectrums of power. Leeken had happily agreed, for a modest fee, of course. So, Jake had the option of what barrel to use at any given time. The point-four barrel had a five-mile range. The Tiban crystal barrels range, according to Leeken was twenty miles or so.

# Anibuna's Office, Madera

"Sir, looking into the recent killings of the hunters has brought up some disturbing intelligence. As you know, we lost all of our hunters in the recent crash. We put out the meteor theory to calm things down and not to spook the real culprits. The impact point on the transport was from underneath. We have kept that fact secret. There's an alarming trend here, sir. The Holinda and the Padenon are both allied with us as you know, and they were also slain by this rogue hunter that appeared so suddenly, and who is left? The scaleslime Hitori and their scaletick ridden partners the Idonax."

"You're right, Kevess! The Hitori hate us. I wondered at the time why they had sent in a team. Well, now we know, and the Idonax scale cleaners will do anything the Hitori ask them to do. They will pay for killing our people. So, it's been these scalerippers that have been killing the other hunters."

"It would seem so, sir. What would you have us do?"

"We uphold the Gishma clan's honour. We kill the scalerotted bangerups. Tell Lunderon we have proof it was the Hitori that killed his nephew. Let the arrogant scaletick do some of the work for us."

# Lunderon's Transport Shuttle

Lunderon reads the message for the third time. His hands crunch into hard fists as he growls at his Thibrans to get the shuttle ready for flight. Revenge awaits.

# Eden Base, Joadin's Office

Zin reads the message from Anibuna's aide Kevess for the third time. Unbelievable. No one had realised, but by pure chance, they had taken out complete factions of Anunnaki at the same time, and the rest were now plotting revenge. Zin shakes his head and is grinning from ear to ear when Ohna walks in.

"Look at this, Ohna. The scale ticks are going to end up fighting amongst themselves. They believe that rival clans are taking each other out. We need to get Willie and Jake in on this. They can stir the pot some more."

"I have been going through the brag-bags we have captured. Good stuff, but again not conclusive proof. What they give us is camouflage if we need to move about down on the planet. We cannot do that without our infiltrators carrying a brag-bag."

She looks over to Duke and Mataoka with a sly grin.

"Why are you looking at me like that, Ohna?" A worried Duke Geneva says.

Mataoka just smiles gently back and nods.

Ohna looks over to Zin and says, "Zin, would you change to Tonvik, please?"

Zin's form starts to shimmer and thirty seconds later, stands an Anunnaki.

"Duke, Mataoka can you copy this Anunnaki?" Ohna asks.

POP! There stand two carbon copies of Tonvik. Ohna hands them wrist comms and the brag-bags and there you have it. The perfect infiltrators so long as no one looked too close or recognised Tonvik. A clever idea from Zin and the application of a couple of swipes with a laz-blade on beaks scarring them gives the pair an individual if slightly intimidating look. Anunnaki chic.

Zin gets permission to land at the Azores Spaceport where the hunters have their individual compounds. Tonvik being a high-ranking Gishma official has demanded he be a part of the investigation into the recent killings. He gets full access to all areas.

The three comrades walk into the first enclosure. There standing up in cages that can let the poor Silvenex do little else are Lunderon's green-dyed and branded hunting dogs. It is obvious from the looks in their multiple eyes that they are fully alert, their minds intact. The trio walk past them quickly and enter the next dome. It's the Hitori Anunnaki's staging area. There is a Blue Silvenex standing in her cage. Drool drips down mandibles and runs down the front of her thorax. Occasional tremors shake her body. Her mind is obviously gone. They quickly stride into the last dome. It belongs to the Idonax. Inside there are two cages sitting side by side. One contains a Blue the other a Black Silvenex missing an arm. One is alert but severely cowed and shrinks back from the three Anunnaki as much as the narrow cage will allow. The other just stands and sways back and forth with foam bubbling at the corners of her mouth.

Zin shakes his head and states, "We need to free these poor Silvenex."

"Why don't we let them decide what they want to do? It's obvious, two are beyond help and the first pair have been mutilated to a point where they could not survive on their own. Let's ask them if they would like to put their sisters out of their misery and take over their bodies."

"Great idea, Mataoka. Let's see if they are willing to do that. Get ready to do your nut-cracking trick, guys."

All three revert to their natural forms. Duke and Mataoka reach into the cages of Lunderon's Silvenex and destroy the slave collar's crystals. Zin explains what the situation with the other Silvenex is like and introduces Mataoka and Duke. Fesdavv and Ouyden. Lunderon's Silvenex ask to speak to their fellow Silvenex first.

All five slip into the next dome. The Blue Silvenex does not react when her collar is destroyed. Ouyden, a fellow Blue, whispers to her broken sister that she will take away her pain and that she will live within her forever.

"I will take your heart straight to heaven, sister, because this body of yours has already been to hell," Ouyden solemnly recites.

POP! The green-tinted body shimmers and disappears and a sleek gunmetal blue body straightens up and walks out of the cage and bows deeply to the three rescuers.

"Thank you. Zin, Mataoka and Duke. I owe you two life debts that I know I will never be able to pay off, lets quickly get poor Fesdavv out of that mangled shell she is in."

They sprint into the last dome. Fesdavv and Ouyden quickly go to talk to the remaining Silvenex. The Blue is broken but desperately wants out of this hell and can't believe the cursed collar is finally off her neck. Her name is Kerasn. Her cage mate Perrix stands mute to their pleas for her to respond. Fesdavv whispers into her poor broken sister's ear slot that she will take away all her suffering. A shimmering pop later and Fesdavv stands whole again with an unmarked jet-black body, minus an arm. She has tears streaming down her face as a multitude of horrific memories get a quick review. All three Silvenex vow bloody revenge.

The six slip out of the compound to the shuttle and streak back to the moon. Fesdavv goes straight to an auto-doc. Several hours later, back at the compound, all hell breaks loose.

"Annnd. There you have it, Games fans. In a daring robbery, all of the competitors' hunting dogs in the Azores compound have been stolen. Games security stated that the cameras in the area had been turned off. It looks to be the work of professional hunting dog thieves, stealing to order. Lunderon of Anisol's prize-winning 'dogs' were probably the intended target of the thieves, and the other three were taken as a bonus. More on this as it develops, Game fans, stay tuned."

Lunderon stands before Anibuna's desk in his palatial home in Madera and demands something is done about the theft. He rants and raves for twenty minutes before he notices the grin on Anibuna's beak. He stops mid-rant.

"Relax, Lunderon. It's been dealt with," sneers Anibuna.

"W-w-what!" stutters Lunderon.

"The Boldonians caught thieves escaping the planet in a converted Slave Harvester, and you know how Boldonians deal with shoplifters."

"Oh damn," sighs Lunderon.

"Yes, Lunderon. They blew it to atoms. Your hunting dogs were insured, of course?"

"Yes, yes, they were, and for a very tidy sum, but that does not stop me from being mad that I did not get to deal with the scale ticks who stole my property," growls Lunderon.

"Never mind. Here, this may cheer you up, it's the location of the Hitori hunting team. They have decided for safety's sake to combine their forces for the last days' hunt."

He slides a set of coordinates across his desk.

"My clan mates were also killed by these scalerippers. So, don't make their ends easy, Lunderon, and as you know, I have three Blues. I will sell you two at a cut-price rate to make up for your losses, and you know my Blues are top-class. What do you say? Do we have a deal?"

Lunderon picks up the coordinates from the desk and holds out his thumb, "Deal."

# San Francisco, USA

The Hitori hunting team for their last big day land on Treasure Island, San Francisco. On request as a last-day favour. Sixty Conpex have been released on the lozenge-shaped island, plus there are rumoured to be some Adamu there as well. The team lands on a pair of large rectangular grass areas bisected by a road. If they had read the sign, it would have said 'Avenue H.' Their Thibrans construct two enclosures encapsulating both grassy parks. Their ship is the smaller of the two with 'Avenue I' running its length. The four friends sit at a table their Thibrans had set up with food and drinks and wait luxuriously while the Thibrans scurry about erecting the energy fences.

The larger park is sectioned into four parts. One for each hunter to display his catches as they bet between themselves about who can catch the most prey. Their single badly abused Blue Silvenex will be shared to help flush out the game. It had been the only Silvenex not in the enclosure when the 'theft' took place.

Dang Lo watches the spaceship come down and land on Treasure Island. This is the second one. The first, the day before had unloaded dinosaurs. There is a green shimmery screen at the end of the Bay Bridge. Some of his gang members had gone to investigate. Ping Hu had lost a hand when he touched it. So, this fence if you like was to keep the dinosaurs in. Good! He had had enough of those things when they had torn through San Francisco months earlier. Tenderloin was a bad enough place to stay. The dinosaurs made it so much worse.

Treasure Island had been blocked by the Games wardens at both exit points so the Conpex could not flee from the island. The standard practice was to give the paying customers what they paid for. A secure hunting area.

Yerba Buena Island has energy fences erected on both sides of it cutting across Interstate Eighty at one end and the Eighty and the Bay Bridge Trail at the other. The Conpex have nowhere to go. Neither have the humans that have returned to the island thinking it was safe. The Conpex hunt in packs of ten or more. They start to prowl the island looking for food.

The Johnstones have lived in Gate view Avenue for years and had never left the island even when the dinosaurs were tearing up San Francisco. Jedidiah had a basement put in the house as it was being built. He is a prepper, and all the complaints he got from his wife Joan and their boys Hank and Frank were now silenced. The boys aged twelve and fourteen are fishing off the rocks beside Perimeter Path. They have caught two Striped Bass and a single Halibut. They were about to call it a day when they heard a low growl coming from down the road towards the Avenue of the Palms. Remembering what their dad had taught them. 'When in doubt…high tail it back home.'

The two boys grab their gear, plus the fish and run the hundred yards across Perimeter Road and onto the grassy back area of the house screaming they had heard dinosaurs. Because once you have heard a dinosaur's roar, you never forget that sound, and the two boys have heard it before. Jed opens the door for them with his AR14 in his hands. Down Perimeter Path, he sees at least five dinosaurs charging towards him.

"Down in the cellar, boys. You know the drill, and don't forget the fish."

They close the heavily reinforced back door and head for the stairs down into the cellar, closing the steel airlock-type door after them. Jed heads quickly to his comms unit and calls his neighbours putting out a warning that the dinosaurs are back. Next, he fires up the outside cameras and the family watch the Conpex sniff about the house trying to get in.

"What about Ma?" Both boys say in unison.

"She'll be fine, boys. She's with her women's meeting showing off her new blue dress she made. I've already given them the heads-up. She'll be okay. Now, get those fish ready. They look tasty."

The Hitori team are ready to go. Each hunter sends up a drone that flies off in different directions. Soon the Thibrans watching the view screens are calling out contact information on various Conpex who are scouring the more populated end of the island looking for food.

With two Thibrans each, the hunters leave the enclosure and separate. Each hunting down his own game. The Thibrans are guiding large grav-carriers with which to carry back captured Conpex. Cronn is the first hunter to see a target. A Conpex is stationary. Munching away at something undefined from Cronn's perspective. He could care less. His target is stationary eighty yards away. He lifts his HIS8 and pulls the trigger. The high-pitched 'Zeeeee' noise from the Mk8 High Impact Stunner shatters the silence.

The Conpex slumps onto its side unconscious. Cronn waves over his Thibrans to put his prize into his section of the enclosure. He walks past a partly eaten Adamu wondering if it is worthwhile using it to lure in another Conpex. He has one of his Thibrans drag it over to Flounder Court and leave it in the middle of its turning circle. Cronn walks across the street to Bigelow Court and sets up his hide and waits to see if the bait brings in another Conpex.

Five minutes later, another Conpex slinks up to the torso and legs of an unknown female Adamu in a bright blue dress and starts to eat it. Cronn lines up the stunner and presses the trigger. Waving his Thibrans forward to collect the stunned creature, he walks back with them to his enclosure. They slide the unconscious reptile inside. The other Conpex is still unconscious and will be for about four hours. He looks at the other three enclosures. They have three times the captives that he has. With a growl of displeasure, he heads back out to get some more. As he is going out, he passes his hunting mates coming in. They all have beak-splitting grins. Their grav-carriers are straining with the weight of multiple Conpex. Cronn just shakes his head and heads back to his chosen hunting area, tail dropping behind him. He has another hour before the allocated time for this part of the bet is up. He manages to bag three more Conpex and in the final count, he is last by a long way.

They now configure the enclosure into three parts; looking down from above it would look like a short-legged T. The bottom of the T is empty and takes up a quarter of the space in the enclosure. The top of the 'T' is split in two. Thibrans are clearing one side of stones and debris. The other has forty-eight still sleeping Conpex in it.

The Hitori had watched the pay-for-view of the mini Games with humans fighting Conpex that the Gishma trio had recorded. Love them or hate them, the Gishma knew how to put on a show, and they had loved it. They were going to do the same for the last day of the hunt. Now they need some Adamu. They are just sitting down to a lunch served by their fawning Thibrans when the unmistakable nasal whine of Lunderon's voice shatters their peace.

# Lunderon

Lunderon landed in a baseball field at the corner of Fourth Street and Avenue N on Treasure Island. He had picked up the Hitori ship and enclosure on his scanner on the way down. He is convinced these scale rippers killed his nephew and sullied Anisol's pride. They will pay for that with their lives.

He leaves his rifle in the shuttle and slips a standard point-two pistol into a holster on his hip. Striding out of his ship, he takes his bearings and walks down Fourth Street until he sees Avenue H. He then turns right and walks towards the glowing green enclosure in the distance. He crosses Ninth Street getting angrier as he walks. Each step rings out with the sharp tap of his cane. In front of him now is Eleventh Street and over to the right in a smaller enclosure is their ship. He walks arrogantly up to the barrier and demands to be let in.

"What in the two hells is that arrogant scaletick doing here, disturbing our hunt?" Rankill snarls.

"Unknown, cousin. Look, he is only armed with a point-two! Would a point-two take down a Conpex?" Nixmal wonders.

"You would need to shoot at point-blank range. Is he that good?" Pzull queries.

"I heard he was," cries Cronn. "Let's see what the scar-faced bangerup wants." Shouting over towards Lunderon, he calls out, "What do you want here, Lunderon? This is not your hunting preserve."

"Your heads! You murdering scaleslime. Face me. I only have a pistol so it should be a fair fight, you useless scaleslime."

The four Hitori hatchmates look at each other and shrug. They have no idea what he is talking about.

"What are you talking about, Lunderon? We never murdered anyone, are you drunk?" Nixmal cries.

"Face me, you cowardly, Hitori scale ticks," screams Lunderon.

"Let's beat the shit out of this arrogant Anisol. They think they are oh, so high and mighty," snarls Pzull.

"Drop the barrier, Rankill, let's hammer this loud-beaked banger up," growls Cronn.

The barrier turns red and the four Hitori angrily stride forward to beat up their single opponent. Lunderon casually lifts his cane as if giving them a wave. The Tiban crystal weapon gives off its deep Wooom four times. It blasts the Hitori to bits. Heads, arms, legs, and guts spray out in an arc, littering the ground behind where they stood with body parts. Some of them eerily twitch for a few seconds before going still.

Lunderon turns his back on the carnage, lifts his tail and pisses on their remains. He walks through the gate to check if any of their hunting gear is worth salvaging. He finds the control for the fences and their blue standing in its cage. It is obvious by its lack of response to him that it is pretty much gone. He presses the control for its shock collar and holds it down. In the cage, the Silvenex bucks and screams until something goes pop! Blood seeps out of its skull as it slowly slides down the bars and falls to the bottom of the cage. Looking around, he notices there are almost fifty Thibrans in a large enclosure next to the now awake and growling Conpex. They can smell the blood. Lunderon goes over to the tables set up for lunch and pulls over a seat. He gets some drinks and settles down to watch the show. With an indifferent push of a button, he opens the gate section between the Thibrans and the Conpex.

"Annnd. There you have it, Games fans. Justice has been done with style and flair. That's an interesting weapon Lunderon used to eliminate the murderers of his nephew Inipan, Games fans. A full unedited recording of the execution of the rogue hunters is available on our pay-per-view channel six. It is well worth the credits. Stay tuned for more as it happens."

# SRC51's Temporary Base
# Jan Mayen Island, Arctic Circle

"Oh, look at this, sisters. Look what that web-snared Anunnaki did to our poor cousin in the cage," sobs Joaxona.

The rest crowd around the screen. All are in shock at the blatant cruelty.

"Play the first bit again, Joaxona," Willie asks softly. "Check out that there walking stick, Jake. Look at the damage it did, and those assholes would have had decent shields. We will need to take this fucker out from a good distance away. Assuming his weapon has the same range as your rifle."

"We need him alive," growls Joaxona. Her voice makes the two snipers' hair stand on end.

"We could try to shoot the stick out of his hand. Then you ladies could administer a little Silvenex-styled justice," drawls Jake.

The Silvenex give them a look that makes their blood run cold. Both snipers shiver involuntarily.

Joaxona nods saying, "Yes, that might work. Let's plan this out, sisters. We have a webworm to trap."

Lunderon now sets his sights on the remaining three Idonax. He is not as sure if they had anything to do with the killing of Inipan but he is going to confront them about it. He knows that while out on the hunt there is no contact with the Games news channel. So, they should not know anything about his hit on their accomplices, the Hitori. He flies out towards the Idonax game reserve.

# Porto Alegre
# Uruguay, South America

Lorrt, Hpsips and Hinpat had picked Farroupilha Park to set up their hunting camp. Their initial scan of the area showed a surprising amount of Adamu. They intend to go out with a bang bagging as many as they can on the last day of the hunt.

Their Thibrans set up the camp and deploy the energy shield in a football field in the eastern corner of a beautifully set out tree-covered park. The three Idonax sit at a table munching on finger food brought out by their fawning servants. They will each take a section of the surrounding densely packed housing areas and hunt individually. With no Silvenex hunting dogs, they revert to using tracking drones. Their Thibrans will monitor the drone's view screens.

Joaxona lands the SRC51 in the northern corner of the Hospital De Clinicas in a little hollow surrounded by trees. The stealth craft fits in neatly. No one sees it land. All eyes are on Lunderon's unsubtle entrance into the area. He lands his harvester scoutcraft just to the side of the Idonax's enclosure. He has no intention of being stealthy. This is going to be an in-your-face approach. He lands almost at the same time as Joaxona unwittingly assisting in her stealthy approach to their target.

Once the SRC lands, Willie and Jake run for the hospital. They make their way up to the hospital's helipad and set up their sniper's perch. Joaxona and her sisters hide in the trees next to the SRC51 and await their chance to get a hold of Lunderon. He is less than three hundred yards away. Meanwhile, Lunderon is striding angrily up to the Idonax's enclosure, walking stick firmly gripped in his right hand.

"Idonax, open this gate! You have questions to answer," growls Lunderon.

The three Idonax hunters look at each other in surprise. It is unheard of in hunting circles to interfere with another hunter's area. What in the two hells is this arrogant scale mould doing demanding entrance to their enclosure?

"Go suck a Thibrans…Never mind. What is it you want, Lunderon? You are spoiling our last day's hunt," shouts Hpsips angrily.

"Let me in. I need to talk to the three of you," demands Lunderon.

"Why?" Lorrt cried holding his hands out from his sides.

"Did you have anything to do with Inipan's death?"

"WHAT!" All three scream at the same time.

"Did you kill my nephew…You scaletick ridden Idonax scum."

"Are you insane, you jumped up, Anisol scalescrubber?" Hinpat growls back.

"Go away, Lunderon, before we send you to ask your precious nephew who did kill him. Because you brain worm-infested scalemould, it was not us," snorts Lorrt.

"Let me in. This is your last warning."

"And you will do what to a point-eight energy fence?" Sneers Hinpat.

"This." Lunderon lifts his walking stick and blows away a complete section of the fence.

Now. That got their attention.

"Woah! Willie, did you see that? The crystal-powered weapon just destroyed that fence." The duo have a clear view of the park from the helipad and are watching events unfold. It is good to see their rifle using the Tiban crystal will be able to slice through an energy fence if necessary.

"Let's watch what happens and then give the girls the word when to move in. You copy that, Joaxona," whispers Jake.

"We are ready…Just say when," snarls an incredibly angry Silvenex.

Lunderon meanwhile has the attention of three very scared Idonax.

"Let me repeat myself, scaleticks. Did you have anything to do with my nephew's death?"

Three heads shake to the negative.

Four of Lunderon's Thibrans carry over a grav-plate. It hovers at waist height. Sitting on it is a brag-bag reader.

"Give me your brag-bags so I can determine the truth."

The three gladly hand over their computers, knowing full well they had nothing to do with any killing.

Lunderon quickly scans the computers and grunts in surprise

"See, Lunderon, we didn't do it! We would never have even considered such a thing," Hinpat spits out.

Both of his partners nod in agreement.

Wooom…Bang! The grav-carrier and the brag-bags explode.

Lunderon quickly turns around lifting up his walking stick to defend himself. It's exactly what Jake had hoped for. His next shot severs the walking stick just below the fancy dark blue crystal nearly taking Lunderon's hand with it.

Willie calls down to the waiting Silvenex screaming, "Go, go, go!"

The grav-cart exploding sends the Idonax reeling backwards. Only Lunderon kept his feet. He soon lands on his back though, as his walking stick explodes. That's where Joaxona finds him as she runs up and delivers a savage kick to his head knocking him unconscious. Xoanona and Loaxona tackle the Idonax. Mere Anunnaki against battle-hardened Blues. No contest. All three hunters get their throats ripped out. They die gurgling on the grass. Joaxona kills the Thibrans with a sweep of her pistol on fully automatic. It is all over in two seconds. They collect the Thibrans and throw them into an undamaged section of the energy fence. They leave the hunters where they lie, for the investigators to find.

Lunderon is webbed up and left beside his harvester craft. Joaxona strides into his ship and hastily searches it for a couple of items. With an evil smile, she returns to her sisters holding up her findings. Her sisters laugh. Yes, that will work. They call Fesdavv and Ouyden who are in Eden Base on the moon and tell them of their plan. The Silvenex look at each other and smile. It's not a pleasant one.

The team gathers up their gear plus the crystal from Lunderon's walking stick which had survived intact. Maybe they can sell it to Leeken. Jake gets Lunderon's triple-barrelled rifle as a trophy. They board the SRC51 and Lunderon's harvester scoutcraft and shoot straight up and head for Eden Base.

## Eden Moon Base

On arriving back at Eden Base, Joaxona seeks out her fellow freed Silvenex. She gives the unconscious Lunderon over to Fesdavv, Ouyden and Kerasn. The three former slaves bow low to Joaxona. With tears of gratitude streaming down their faces, they take Lunderon away to their quarters on the base. The doors are quite thick, as they need to act as an airlock in times of emergencies. Once the doors are closed, they are quite soundproof. This is just as well because slave training is a noisy business.

# Lunderon

Lunderon awakens to strange surroundings. He is standing in a tall, narrow, one-yard square, wire-mesh cage that he can barely move inside. His beak hurts terribly, and his bionic eye is offline. He manages to slide one arm up to explore his painful face. His hand pulls away in shock. He finds a round smooth bump where his razor-sharp beak should be. His eye patch is also missing, and around his throat is a collar with a large crystal fixed to it. Lunderon starts to scream.

The three former slaves move in. Cattle-prods crackle in anticipation of the use they will soon be engaged in. Lunderon starts to scream in earnest.

# Anibuna's Mansion Madera

"Annnd there you have it, Games fans," Sparyten's wide smiling beak fills the screen. "In an explosive end to Anibuna Nineties' inaugural hunt, the rogue hunters have all been slain by Lunderon of the Anisol, and in typical Lunderon fashion, he has left us to wonder what exactly happened here on Thera Three, and how he managed to take down three very experienced hunters without using a weapon? This all adds to the illusive hunter's mystique. Unfortunately, our overhead satellite covering that area was malfunctioning so there is no video of his last kills, other than what the Games adjudicators found on the scene."

"Now that footage is available on our pay-for-view channel six, and let me tell you, gentle beings, it was not a pulse weapon he used to kill the rogue hunters. It was his claws! Unedited footage from the Games adjudicators' investigation is a must-see. Viewer discretion is advised. Lunderon's harvester craft took off this morning and headed for orbit and a slingshot around Thera Three's satellite to parts unknown. We will surely see him for the next hunt." The camera pans out showing a smiling Anibuna. Sparyten continues with his interview.

"So, Anibuna Ninety, your hunt has been a spectacular success. Our feedback from our galactic audience survey was in the high eighty per cent. Well done, sir. What is next, may I enquire for our audience?"

The camera pans over and Anibuna preens in its glow. His head crest is fully erect showing his display feathers.

"Well, Sparyten, we will put in a few changes after the business of the rogue faction within the hunters shows up. We will make the new hunts clan-specific. So, only one clan will hunt at any one time. This will not stop the usual clan rivalries taking place, of course, we expect that as a natural course of events."

"That seems a good course of action," says Sparyten in his serious voice.

"Yes, it is, isn't it? To show we don't do favourites. The Gishma clan is not in the draw for the first hunt."

"That is very generous, and you are going to draw the winning clan right now on the Games channel?"

"Yes, Sparyten. Would you like to do the honours?" Anibuna slides a bowl made from a polished human skull across to the announcer. It's filled with strips of colourful paper.

"I would be delighted." Sparyten digs in a manicured claw picking out a ticket; he hands it to Anibuna.

"Our first individual clan hunt goes to theee," Anibuna stretches out the suspense for a few seconds, "Hitori."

"Excellent. You saw it here first, Games fans. The first thousand hunters will be exclusively from the Hitori clan, and the date will be? When has the next hunt been scheduled for, Anibuna Ninety?"

"In two weeks, Sparyten. We are waiting for more animals to be brought in to restock losses. Then we will open the doors."

"Splendid. Well, Games fans, stay tuned for more as it unfolds. This has been Sparyten for the Games channel. Happy hunting."

# Lunderon

Lunderon stands trembling in his new cage. It's five yards square and has bars from top to bottom. He is covered in little round burn marks from his three mistresses, the application of the powerful cattle-prods. They have not used the shock collar yet. That will change today.

Fesdavv orders Lunderon to sit.

Lunderon does nothing but glares at his tormentor and sneers as much as his ruined beak will allow.

Fesdavv presses a button on a handheld remote and pain like Lunderon has never experienced in his life knifes through his brain. He sits. This goes on for a week. Then he is transferred to a ten-yard circular cage with an eight-foot-high metal spike in the centre. A lead goes from the spike to Lunderon's collar. He is made to go in circles, change direction, stop, turn left and right, made to jump, sit, run, walk and lie down. All the commands are screamed at him. Any hesitation at all sees him dropping to the ground and curling up into a foetal position as he is lashed by the collar. He stays like that until the pain goes away. This is done non-stop for days. Each one of the former slaves took her turn at being the pony trainer.

# Thera Three
# Australian Outback

A huge enclosure is constructed. The fence posts for the mile-square habitat disappear in the distance. It lights up the desolate area around Lake Cohen in the Gibson Desert with a green flickering sheen. Into this enclosure are dumped two thousand Limies. These little predators breed like Thibrans and hunt in packs of hundreds. Their small mouths are full of razor-sharp teeth. They overwhelm and shred their prey down to the bare bone in seconds. These are feared in the Games. Any adversary has to be fast and be able to kill the little devils before being torn to pieces.

The crowds have loved them. The Games procurement team caught a hundred or so white fluffy-looking four-legged herbivores. They drop them into the enclosure. Immediately, every Limies head rises as they sniff the meaty smell of the sheep. Then acting as if they are one organism, they surround and envelope their frightened prey. A rending noise is heard above the terrified bleats of the sheep as the buzzsaw mouths of the Limies destroy the poor animals. Within forty seconds, nothing is left but scattered bone and puffs of wool.

# Eden Base Control Room

The entire team is reunited for the first time in months. There is an almost party atmosphere as the teams mix and renew acquaintanceships.

Zin calls everyone to order and starts laying out ideas to stop the hunting, and eventually free the Earth from the Anunnaki.

"Okay, our elimination of the Anunnaki Games on Yona is complete, and the planet is now thriving under Olkon and Fumil's leadership. They've also set up a rehabilitation area where former collared slaves can be treated and offered a safe place to stay. Unfortunately, the bloodthirsty Anunnaki have started this hunting business on Earth, and by all accounts, it is worse than the original Games. We need to stop this without involving the Belatan Peacekeeping Force. We cannot survive against the Andrend Poltox without bringing in Alliance strength and firepower. So, everything has to be done by stealth."

"The quick fix would be for one of us to subsume Anibuna, and through him stop the hunting, but he is a paranoid scale tick and is covered by some advanced weaponry and security measures. We have just heard that they have invented a scanner that can detect a shapeshifted individual. They are fitting these at every security post on the planet. I also heard that they may be portable. So, we will need to be very careful. Infiltration will need to be subtle. Any ideas."

Fesdavv, Ouyden and Kerasn walk forward. Fesdavv speaks for the three of them.

"Would Lunderon be any good at gaining entry to Anibuna? We know Anibuna offered to sell Lunderon two of his Blues." She nods over to where Joaxona and her sisters are standing. "Now what kind of damage could you three do in the same room as that webworm?" Her grin is downright evil. "We just need to do some cosmetic work on our pet, Lunderon and he is ready to perform."

"I knew you ladies had been given Lunderon, but I thought you had just killed the scale tick."

"No, no, no. Zin, that would have been way too easy on him. We did much more than that. We turned the web-slime into our slave. He'll now do anything we say. He has gotten to fear the shock collar as much as any of us did. He's completely under its influence."

"That will do the trick. Do what you need to do to make this work, Fesdavv." Turning to face the other Silvenex, Zin grins saying, "Joaxona, dig out your Thibran collars. It's time for you to go back to your 'Master'."

Lunderon is put into an auto-doc and his beak is repaired. His eyepatch is refitted with something that looks like Silvenex chitin and a clever bit of surgery inserts his shock collar crystal into his neck hiding it from view.

Lunderon is ordered to sit in front of a communications plate and is hooked up to speak to Anibuna. He has a script he is to read. The call goes through.

Anibuna looks at the incoming call screen and is surprised to see it is Lunderon. He hits the accept button.

"Anibuna Ninety, have you forgotten about my Blues? Give me your price and I will collect them at your convenience."

"We thought you had left, Lunderon."

"No, I merely wished to be away from that scalelicker Sparyten. When can I get my Blues?"

"As soon as they are back with me, Lunderon. They had a task to complete. I am waiting for them to finish that and then you may make your choice of whichever of the three you wish. You may have the pair for two million credits which as you know is well under their worth. All three are high-quality stock and have been fully trained. You pick which ones you prefer."

"Excellent, let me know when I can come to view them. I will come down to your island and await my Blues' arrival."

"I will retrieve them today and have them cleaned and ready for your inspection."

"See that you do, Anibuna."

Click! Lunderon switches off the connection. Just behind him, Fesdavv whispers, "Good boy," into his ear.

Anibuna calls Joaxona, "Stop what you are doing, Silvenex and return to my island immediately. I take it the Koban are no longer a problem."

Joaxona answers immediately, "The Koban have been destroyed, Master. We need to find transport back to you."

"Do it immediately. No excuses or you will feel my displeasure."

"Immediately, Master. We will leave within the hour."

"See that you do," growls Anibuna, unconsciously mimicking Lunderon's previous call.

The three Blues wearing their Thibran collars, plus Wang and Flash, jump into the SRC51. Brakk flies them down to Earth. She lands unseen in the Randorian Embassy compound. Flash and Wang volunteered to be her human pilots for the corporate jet which had been left parked in a hangar near the embassy. After a quick pre-flight check, they troop into the jet and head for Madera.

Anibuna's luxury mansion is in Funchal. The beautiful house overlooks the sea. He is sitting by the pool with a large glass of red wine in his hand, its glass straw catching the sunlight awaiting the return of his Blues. His Thibrans hover about awaiting his every wish. Hearing a craft in the sky, he looks up to see Lunderon's distinctive harvester scoutcraft head towards the nearby airport in Santa Cruz that had been converted into a usable spaceport. It also houses the Belatan Peacekeeping Forces Security Station.

The Andrend Poltox set up their dome at the Estrada De Santa Catarina end of the single runway. Their dome completely obscured the large 05 painted on it. All visitors go through spaceport security before they can enter Madera and from there, any city on the island. They are using the new shapeshifter scanner developed by Doplon for the first time.

Flash radios in for permission to land and is given it. He is told a transport grav-skimmer will pick up Anibuna's property after they land and go through security. The 'Adamu' are told to stay in the aircraft. Flash acknowledges the transmission. He nods over to Wang and snorts, "Now there's a fellow that's dedicated to his job…Asshole." Wang just grins.

Lunderon's harvester has already landed. He is waiting for permission from Fesdavv to leave the craft and make his way to see Anibuna. He has already been checked over by two of the Poltox security detail and had a scanner waved over him. A solid tone sounded from the scanner showing the individual is who he seems to be. It gives a warbling alarm if it detects a shifted being inhabiting the body.

Joaxona and her sisters also pass through security without any issues. She calls Anibuna and informs him they are at the airport. Anibuna replies telling the Silvenex to go to the grav-skimmer which will take them up to his mansion. At the same time, a taxi stops at Lunderon's ship, and the driver announces he is here to take him to see Anibuna. Fesdavv tells him to go with the driver and then to take orders from any of the Silvenex in Anibuna's presence.

# Anibuna's Mansion, Madera

Joaxona and her sisters are ushered away by Anibuna's Thibrans to an outside shower and are thoroughly washed and then given a light coating of polish to show off their sleek gunmetal bodies. They are told to wait. A Thibran will usher them in when the time is right.

Lunderon walks up to Anibuna's door and a Thibran shows him through to the pool where Anibuna is waiting.

"Ah, Lunderon, so good to see you. Take a seat, do you wish something to eat or drink?"

"No, thank you, Anibuna Ninety. Let's just get to business. Where are my Blues?"

Anibuna lifts one hand and away runs a Thibran to collect the Silvenex.

Joaxona and her two sisters walk into the small pool courtyard and stand meekly in a line beside Anibuna. He stands and waves his hands proudly towards his Blues.

"Well, Lunderon, did I not say they were first class? Come and examine them if you like, but I can assure you that they are in fine condition."

Lunderon uses both hands to lift Joaxona's head displaying the crystal at her throat.

"These crystals will need to be replaced. This one has small cracks at the side, look."

Anibuna absentmindedly hands his brag-bag to the nearest Thibran and lifts Joaxona's head with both hands mimicking Lunderon. He peers at the crystal. It's exactly what they hoped he would do…Bang! Anibuna gets head-butted by Joaxona. Her rock-hard chitin skull hits him like a hammer. He drops to the polished marble floor with a smack, unconscious. Joaxona quickly cocoons him in the web and drags him into the house. Lunderon follows her in like a puppy. Xoanona and Loaxona then hunt down and shoot all of the Thibrans in the building dumping their bodies unceremoniously in a laundry room. Using her wrist com, Joaxona calls for an extraction from the SRC51. There is room for it to land in the gardens beside the large house. The pair in the corporate jet is told to leave and head back to the Randorian Embassy. Mission accomplished.

Joaxona grabs all of Anibuna's personal gear plus his brag-bag. He has a lot of explaining to do. She can hear the downwash of the stealth craft rattle off the courtyard walls. It's time to go. She carries Anibuna kicking and screaming into the SRC51. They shoot straight up, breaking the atmosphere and head straight for Eden Base. Lunderon and the two Blues calmly order a taxi back to the spaceport where they go through the exiting protocols and depart from the spaceport and head for the moon.

Anibuna is put into one of the Poltox interrogation cells while Lisle and Shoull put his brag-bag on a reader and do an electronic version of the same thing. They just don't use a shock collar as motivation.

# Anibuna's Conquest Ship
# The Anun

The communications officer looks up to the command chair. Holding up his hand to his earpiece, as he listens to another negative response.

"What is it, Dewsun?" Wolknun, the ship's captain asks.

"Sir, Lord Anibuna has now missed three scheduled reporting time slots. I am required to inform you of this. His next scheduled report is in ten minutes."

"You have tried to contact him I take it." A slight growl of impatience crept into his voice.

"Yes, sir. Right after the first missed communication slot."

"Hmm! It's not like Anibuna to miss a contact."

"He has missed a few recently, sir. When I call down, his Thibrans always tell me he is indisposed, but if it is really important, they will try to get him to respond?"

"Ahh! Yes." Thinking to himself that Anibuna is getting a little too fond of the planet's alcohol. "*Get my shuttle ready. I will go down and see him myself.*"

"Immediately, sir." The comms operator turns back to his console to call down to the hangar deck.

Wolknun and three security specialists plus half a dozen Thibrans march into the hangar bay. The pilot is standing by the open side door to the shuttle. He salutes as Wolknun approaches and asks what their destination is to be. Wolknun returns the cross-body salute and tells the pilot to take them down to Anibuna's mansion on Thera Three.

The pilot gets permission to depart and clearance from the Belatan blockade commander that it is okay to proceed down to Anibuna's mansion. This will be Wolknun's first time on the planet. His crew have been getting regular shore leave to the Azores Spaceport, but he has always been too busy up to this point to indulge, so seeing his commander is just the right excuse. The shuttle lands at Santa Cruz spaceport and a ground skimmer is commandeered. It has a grav-trailer fitted. The Thibrans are shoved into the trailer. They fly around the island following the coast until they come upon Funchal. The autopilot unerringly lands them in the courtyard of Anibuna's mansion. Where are the Thibrans?

The nosey inquisitive servants are usually awaiting any new arrivals that come to any Anunnaki's dwelling. If for nothing else but to direct their visitors to their master's whereabouts.

The Thibrans are let out of the trailer. They immediately start to wail, becoming very agitated and afraid.

"Find out what's bothering the Thibrans Hrveras."

"Yes, sir. Immediately."

His security team leader grabs a Thibran by its harness and drags it towards the house. Screaming in its ear slot to stop acting like a Durgo lizard and find its fellow Thibrans.

Kollive smelt the blood of the dead Thibrans as soon as the trailer was opened. He is terrified of what he might find, but his terror of the large burly security specialist overrides his fear of what might have happened to his counterparts. He follows his nose to the mansion's laundry room. His little hand goes up to his mouth in fright. Hrveras draws out his point-two pistol and calls the rest of his security team to cover the XO. He systematically searches the area before racing back to report to Wolknun what he's found.

The security specialists search the mansion. There are no signs of a struggle. Nothing is missing. There is no blood and no Anibuna? Did he kill his Thibrans in a fit of rage? It's not unheard of. They return to the shuttle leaving the Thibrans to deal with their fallen brethren and head back to the spaceport. Questioning the Poltox security commander just throws up more questions.

There have only been two craft that arrived and departed the spaceport. It's all on film. The security officer shows them Lunderon and his recently bought Blues go through security screening before taking off. The Adamu never left their small jet. They had been kept under surveillance the entire time. Anibuna is a well-known recognisable figure on the island. He should still be here. Because he never left according to all the scanners and radar employed by the Poltox. Are they sure they looked everywhere?

Exasperated. Wolknun calls up to the ship and tells them to shuttle down two hundred Thibrans. He will have them search the entire island if it comes to it. He has a bad feeling that something terrible has happened to Anibuna.

# Eden Base Security Cells

Anibuna has not told them anything so far even after being shocked several times by the collar he now wears around his neck. He knows they will not subsume him for the information in his head about the Gishma's dealings with Thera Three. A subsumed being's testimony is not admissible in the Belatan court system, and his brag-bag will soon delete itself if it is out of his hands for any length of time without his special security input code. He just needs to get out of here and onto a transport of any kind. Suddenly a terrible commotion is heard at the bottom of the cell block and a scuffing sliding noise finally reveals a badly battered Joadin, who is thrown unceremoniously into the cell across from Anibuna.

The recording devices in the cells are running. Anibuna starts to call out in a panicked voice to Joadin asking him if he is all right and does he have any idea what's happening to them. Cydon aka Joadin just groans through the clever make-up and closes his eyes.

Anibuna is starting to sweat.

Back in the Workshop Lisle and Shoull, both scream out a string of colourful profanities as Anibuna's brag-bag smoulders as the delicate matrix inside it goes up in flames.

They never so much as got one iota of information from the thing. The liberation of Earth through legal means is reliant on getting a confession out of Anibuna to overturn the Belatan court's ruling. All they have up until this point is forwarded to Randor.

# Randor
# SID Main Office

"Quin, look at this! Zin, that special envoy they have on Earth has captured the Gishma's troubleshooter Anibuna." Reading the screen, he grunts in disappointment. "Unfortunately, he had his computer set up to purge itself if a signal was not sent to it at a predetermined time." He looks at his long-time partner in the Randorian Government Special Investigations Department (SID) and grins. They have Anibuna.

"We can squeeze that scale tick until he bursts. This is the first top-echelon Gishma we have gotten our hands on. We need to get in there before the locals make a mess and totally rip the scales off the entire thing," SID Officer Jetroll enthuses.

They immediately organise a fast courier craft to go to the Anunnaki base on Earth's moon, to professionally deal with Anibuna. They even have their own thumb screws.

# Eden Base

Zin looks up from the comms panel and grimaces. They are getting a SID unit to oversee the interrogation of Anibuna. He can still recall his dealings with the sadistic scale ticks when he was in Parvon training. The SID conducted the dreaded Escape and Evasion Training for the Parvon personnel. They were not gentle in their approach. He calls back and asks to speak to Randorian Supreme Court officer Tinan.

"Ohna!" calls Zin. Ohna looks up from the screen she was studying. "What was the name of that scalemould SID trainer we had for E-n-E?"

"Emm, Zunn, I think."

"Yep, that was the scaleripper's name. Zunn."

# Parvon Training Ground on Randor's Second Moon Kessron 2AIA

Zin is in the second year of his seven-year Parvon training. He's still getting used to his soon-to-be mate, Ohna. A feisty female that Zin is not sure about at all. The powers-to-be select them both as a perfect match. He just can't see it. She's so bossy. She keeps picking him up on things he would forget. Like right now, he's supposed to report to some pen-pusher from the SID to get his Escape and Evasion Training signed off. He and Ohna had been dropped in the middle of the training moon's jungle area with minimal survival equipment. The two of them had aced it. He even impressed his hard-to-impress partner with his ability to build shelters and traps.

It's been two years since the Koban mother left Randor in the throes of a planet-wide Ice Age. He looks up and can see the solid white ball of Randor float above him in the early evening sky. Even now, two years later, it still brings a lump to his throat. He lost a lot of hatch mates when Randor went into its Ice Age. Shaking off the feeling, he looks around to see where the blasted female's gone. They were supposed to meet in this building. Now where in the two hells is his partner Ohna?

Just at that, the lights go out!

Zin awakens, strapped to a sturdy chair in a dark room. In front of him is a view screen showing Ohna strapped to a similar chair. There is blood on her face. A lot of blood. It's running down her cheek and dripping onto her leg before running down and forming a little puddle by her left foot.

The questions start. What is your name? What is your identification number? What is the security number to get access to the base?

A hefty electric shock at every question makes his spine twist. He gives out an involuntary groan at each shock.

The questions re-start.

This goes on for what seems like hours until suddenly, there is a change of tactics.

"If you fail to answer our questions, the female will be killed." On the screen, an arm comes into view holding a standard point two-phase pistol, which is pointed directly at Ohna. A white bag is then pulled over her head, obscuring it from view.

"You have five beats to answer my questions," growls the unseen interrogator.

"One, two, three, four."

Zin sits, looks at the screen then shrugs. Hell, he didn't even like the female too much. So, through clenched teeth, he tells his interrogator to shove his tail up his ass.

"Five!"

Pop! The white bag covering Ohna's head blossoms with orange blood. She slumps forward against the restraints.

Huh! he actually felt sorry that the short-tempered, caustic female was gone. Who would have thought?

The lights come on and a technician comes in and releases him. Standing in the doorway is Zunn, resplendent in his white interrogator's harness. "Well done, trainee Zin. That concludes your Escape and Evasion Training, report to trainer Zim for further instructions as to the next part of your course."

"Excuse me, sir. What of Ohna? Will I get a new partner?"

"The execution was staged, trainee Zin."

"Oh! It was very convincing. Did Ohna let me die as well?"

"Yes, not only did she let you be killed to save her secrets but she was smiling as it happened. Good luck with that one security specialist, Zin. You will need it."

Zin smiles at the memory.

"What are you smiling about?" Grins Ohna.

"Just thinking back to the E-n-E training where you got shot in the head."

"That was so obviously fake. No one with half a brain would have fallen for that one," scoffs Ohna.

"I know, right," lies Zin.

# Thera Three
# Games Procurement Stevedores

"Are you sure the two hundred Limies are to be put into this area, Hervenn?"

"Yep, says it right here. Area Seven! Limie Encounter Zone. Grade four hunters and above only."

"Okay, but they usually put these little devils onto an island, or an area blocked by an energy fence," waving his arms in a big circle. "This place is wide open. If they don't kill all the little scalerippers, they will breed like Thibrans."

"True, but what's the worry? They can't get to you if you have your shield switched on. Even a cheap point-one shield is enough, Joopss. So, don't worry about it, it's well above our pay grade. What's next, the Conpex, right."

Joopss gives him a patronising look saying, "You know that's crap, don't you?"

"What?"

"Limies are immune to personal shield energies. Why do you think we get more credits for handling the little scale ticks?"

"What! We were told our shields would protect us from the Limies."

"Who told you that! Nope, they slice through a point-eight as if it wasn't there."

"By the two hells. I wasn't told that. Let's get out of here. What's next? The Conpex, right."

Looking at his tablet, Joopss answers, "Yes. Forty Conpex in Section Ten. Then we have twelve Janarks and Nomals for area fourteen and we are done for today. A purple beer awaits at Stex's Bar." Joopss loves winding his partner up. Thank Gangin, the Limies aren't immune to the fences.

"Sounds good and the first paying hunt is on the weekend. I thought we'd be out of a job when the Games fell apart. This is as good a deal as we had back with Kollexx."

"That's a fact, Hervenn, and it will be good to see fellow Hitori again. Let's finish up quickly. That beer is looking real good right now."

# The Hollers
# Harlan County, Kentucky

Harlan County's been quiet for the last six months. The dinosaurs all died off and the power is back on. Bubba Wilks never came back to reclaim his survivalist shelter, so Frank Watts and his family settled in. Kyle even got a hold of a puppy from a local farmer and is teaching it how to be a good sheepdog. Everything's good. That goodness is shattered when a large spaceship overflew the house and lands at the airport just north of Loyall which on Hervenn's data pad said area seven. This is the second spaceship to land in Harlan. The first one landed down by the National Guard Building two months ago and did nothing other than erect a big green dome over itself and just sit there with a guard at a protected doorway. It never bothered them, so they never bothered it.

Frank immediately calls the sighting into the local Harlan militia that had been formed to deal with the dinosaurs originally, but now it's to deal with marauding biker gangs that had shown up and were terrorising survivalist communities for food and fuel. Their treatment of any females they find is barbaric no matter what age they are. Bikers are usually shot on sight.

Hell's Harvesters is a greasy bunch of bikers who had originally been rival biker gang members until the dinosaurs came. They band together and travel from place to place, surviving by plundering their way through every small town they come across. There are forty-three of them. Not counting five badly abused women in a cage-covered trailer that is towed by a massive three-wheeler bike that the gang leader Rankin drives. They are screaming down Highway 119 looking for weed grown in the local hollers. Slick Dan, one of his lieutenants, heard there's some primo-weed in Shoemaker Hollow, near Harlan. So, they are going to check it out.

The trailer bed is six feet by eight and is four feet high. Originally, it was for transporting hay bales and the like. Now it has five women crammed inside it. They hate, hate, hate, the cage with a vengeance.

Deadeye, the biker point man sees something. Up ahead on the left is a vet hospital. He peels off the highway and stops by its front door; kicking down the stand, he dismounts the bike. Vet hospitals have been good places to find drugs. The rest of the gang peel into the parking lot and conduct a well-practised search of the hospital. Cages inside contain dead animals that have starved to death when the hospital was abandoned all those months back. The hardened bikers don't give them a second glance.

Amy, the youngest of the bikers captives, is the first to hear the weird chirping noise. It seems to come from everywhere. Then she sees a small dog-sized dumpy reptile sitting looking at her with big eyes. It looks quite cute. Its head raises and sniffs the air. Its chirps get more frantic. All of a sudden, there are what seems like hundreds of little

Hadrosaurus-looking reptiles scurrying around them. The women huddle closer as they climb onto the trailer. Their little mouths try to get to them through the mesh.

The captives get a close-up look at their meat-grinding teeth before they all jump off, and quickly enter the building attracted by the high-pitched screams from within, or it was maybe the smell of blood. The bikers caught in the confined space inside the hospital have nowhere to go. They are overwhelmed. The small sharp teeth tear into bikie leathers and soon reach the succulent flesh underneath. It's over in minutes. Not a shred of flesh is left on the bones, and every drop of blood is lapped off the tiled floor.

The five women in the cage watch the little mini dinosaurs run out of the building and disappear. The cage door is just held closed by a simple latch. They open it and crawl out of the hated cage and start looking nervously about. It's just what the cunning little predators were waiting for. The women are surrounded and attacked from all sides. Each little bite is the same as a human eating an apple. A crescent-shaped chunk of flesh is torn away and consumed by the constantly ravenous Limies. The screaming women would give anything to be back in their hated cage again.

Harlan County emergency and rescue station is being used by the militia as a command base. It has radios and vehicles which all now work and as they overlooked the airport, they actually saw the spaceship land and dump off a load of small unconscious reptiles. They just left them lying on the runway tarmac. They radio the police station on Carter Road which is manned by volunteer militia to go check it out.

The police cruiser that drove onto the runway found no trace of the little dinosaur-like things. The two men just shrug;

what kind of damage could a few hundred knee-high little reptiles do? They report that the area is secure. The creatures have all gone.

# Polyrend Four
# Second Arm of the Spiral Galaxy

The home planet of the Limies is typical of the planets closer to the galactic centre. It's mostly arid with a few shallow seas and inland lakes. The plant life is hardy, and the animals were either reptilian or insectoid. Limies are small burrowing reptiles way down the food chain. They are the staple diet of most of the bigger reptiles and a couple of the larger insects. Limies live in massive underground warrens and hunt in large groups for protection. Food eaten can be regurgitated later for their young and the Limies that stay to protect the nest. Female Limies are almost constantly pregnant delivering broods of eight to twelve young every four months. If the predation wasn't as good as it is, then the Limies would have overrun the planet years ago.

And now they are on Earth. With no natural predators whatsoever. What could possibly go wrong?

# Eden Base Hangar Deck

The Randorian SID team stride arrogantly down the gangplank and walks over to the waiting group of mixed beings. There are only two Randorians among them. Immediately, Quinn tries to insert himself as the leader and sneers at Zin and Ohna saying that they will now take over the interrogation. They can watch if they want to learn something useful. His sidekick grins evilly over his shoulder. Zin does not bat an eyelid which for a Randorian is side to side. He simply hands the sanctimonious scale tick a communicator which has Supreme Judge Tinan on the other end. Watching a Randorian go pale with shock is a wonderful thing to see.

Quinn's tail which had been standing proudly erect in line with his spine is now lying limp on the floor behind him. His throat pouch which had been puffed out slightly is now flat against his chest. With a slightly trembling hand, he returns the communicator to Zin. Ohna leans in until her snout is almost touching Quinn's ear and whispers, "Try anything like that again and we will drop you on the planet. OUR! interrogation got US information that they are seeding the planet with Limies. You and your scaletick of a partner can go down and verify that for us, or you can draw in your ego and scalescrubbing help us without the scaleripping attitude!"

Quinn just nods.

Zin gives them a hard look and says, "So, here's what we have been doing. The Poltox commander subsumed the top scientist here who happens to be Anibuna's partner in the whole thing…"

Jetroll buts in saying, "You know, we can't use any of his testimony."

"We know that! Durgo brain," sneers Ohna.

Zin gives them another hard look saying. "We have him in the cell next to Anibuna with audio and video running twenty-four-seven."

The two SIDs share a glance and nod. "That's a pretty good idea. You should have been a SID officer."

The look of disgust on Zin's face actually made the pair blush.

"What kind of information are you getting out of the scale tick? Quinn and I have been after this piece of scalemould for years. We only want to see this piece of Durgo crap spend time on Quanteral prison planet and hopefully bring down the entire Gishma for good. So, no more scalebuffing. We are here to help. Let's peel every scale off this bangerup and finish this."

Anibuna is dragged out of his cell and brought into an interrogation room. The two SIDs introduce themselves, showing the distinctive shield with the SID logo on it. Anibuna visibly pails. The SIDs are known galaxy-wide for their ruthless methods of getting justice done. What he did not expect was an apology.

"We are so sorry about this, Lord Anibuna. Ambassador Zin overstepped his authority. We will return you to your house on Thera Three as soon as we conduct our investigation into Ambassador Zin. Would you be willing to be interviewed so we can bring a case about the ambassador's blatant disregard of Belatan jurisprudence? We hope to strip him of his title. He may even end up on Quanteral. This is a serious matter. Again, please accept our apologies. We will have this dealt with as soon as possible. You will find some of the Adamu's wine in your room and some food. Please accept this as a small part of our apology."

A confused Anibuna is led back to his cell. Joadin is sitting with his head in his hands moaning slightly. He looks up saying, "Did they beat you, Anibuna? I heard the SID scale rippers could be brutal."

"No, old friend. It's Zin they are after." He pours himself a large glass of red wine. Taking a large sip from the straw attached to the glass, he gloats saying, "We are in the clear."

"What about?" Joadin says nervously, looking left and right. "You know?"

"They know nothing about you manipulating the Belatan judge or me instigating the release of your modified Koban. We are free and clear to continue to strip this planet bare." He quickly finishes the bottle. There are several in the crate. The recorders don't miss a thing.

Glued to the surveillance screen, Jetroll cries out in delight saying, "Quin, we have the bangerup dead to rights. We have it all."

Quinn looks at his grinning partner saying, "Let's get this information to head office, Jetroll." They try the comms unit. It's unresponsive. A diagnostics scan shows the system is down due to a solar flare. It's predicted to last at least a week.

They will have to take the information themselves. An evil smile passes between them. They can spin this showing they were the ones to crack Anibuna. The pair go tell Ohna and Zin about the solar flare. Jetroll starts his spiel. His words are so obviously insincere; it's embarrassing. He tells them that they will be given an equal share of the kudos when *they* deliver the evidence to Randor.

Zin and Ohna watch the SID pair streak out of the hangar knowing full well they will claim responsibility for gaining the data on Anibuna. Screw them. The team on the moon must keep up their subterfuge. Anibuna's disappearance must be explained. A story is put out about Joadin bringing him up to the moon using one of the small Thibran harvester crafts after a drunken misadventure in his mansion. He is helping him detoxify his body. Why the Poltox did not record their departure? They can only surmise their equipment was faulty.

# Gishma Leadership Complex, Planet Bleopan

"Our spy in the Randorian SID has some troubling news, Dovernn One," reports Jintol.

"Must I wait for it." Snaps the Gishma clan's chieftain.

"S-sorry, sir, it seems Anibuna Ninety and Joadin One have compromised the mining enterprise on Thera Three. The SID is bragging they have evidence to counter the Belatan ruling and are waiting on the Randorian legal team to put in the evidence to rescind the ruling. Our legal team think they will succeed." Gulps the Chieftain's long-suffering aide

"Arrrg! How did they manage that? Where is Anibuna?"

"Still on Eden, sir. It seems he is being treated for alcoholism by Joadin. That may explain how information slipped out. Or we may have a spy sir."

"Contact the GSS about that. What are our options, Jintol?"

"We can distance ourselves from Anibuna and lay the entire thing on him as a rogue operator overstepping his boundaries, or we send in a fleet and back him up until we strip the planet bare."

"How long is the estimate on what's left of Thera Three's resources?"

"Two hundred years, sir, at the present mining rate. The Adamex are very efficient."

"Humm, that's too much to let go. What is the Belatan presence in the system?"

"One intimidator class battleship and a full Maxus brood group of Andrend Poltox."

"So, we are looking at a quarter of a million, Andrend."

"Yes, sir, and as you know, the Andrend are enhanced. They are almost twice as fast and stronger than a regular Poltox."

"This hunting venture that Anibuna conceived. He had Limies, did he not?"

"Yes, he did, sir. Thousands of them," Grins Jintol catching his chieftain's line of thought.

If Poltox fear one thing, it's Limies. It had taken years for the savage little creatures to be eradicated from the Poltox home world, where they had been introduced as a fast-breeding food source during a time of severe food shortages. It had gone terribly wrong. The Limies started to see the Poltox as a threat and would attack them in a feeding frenzy. The quick-breeding Limies soon became a worldwide problem as whole communities were overwhelmed and eaten.

It had gotten to a point of desperation so bad that a radical idea from a scientist ended up creating a super soldier Poltox. The Andrend clan volunteers to be experimented on with drugs initially, and then surgical enhancements to be able to finally rid the little horrors from the planet. Once the infestation is eradicated, the Andrend are shamefully shunned by the other Poltox as being too different. Too superior in themselves. Fighting amongst the Poltox becomes so bad that the Alliance come in and stops it.

In an act of reconciliation, the Andrend are given a virgin planet to colonise. They name it Haven. It's on the outskirts of Belatan space. The entire clan splits from the rest of the Poltox and becomes almost another species. The mistrust and betrayal by the normal Poltox are deeply ingrained in the Andrend. They have little or no contact with their fellow Poltox. They put their entire culture into the service of the Belatan Banking and Legal Guilds. They were the only civilisation that had not treated them like freaks. Showing them kindness and monetary support until the community started to flourish. As a result of this and by way of a thank you, they started to offer their services to the Banking Guild as debt recovery agents, and it just spiralled from there. A very strong mutual bond had been forged between the two vastly different cultures.

"Have the Limies scattered around the Poltox barracks. They should hold their attention and take their claws away from our mining enterprises. Order Anibuna's ship to destroy the Belatan battleship. Make sure it does not send out a distress call. Reinsert the suppression web satellites to lock down our possessions on the planet. Contact Feydon. Send in his fleet of scale rippers to defend our possessions. Once the Belatans are out of the way, give the Boldonians a passage up to their orbital warehouse. That should keep those money-hungry scaleticks happy. We do not want to mess with the storekeepers." Grins Dovernn One.

Jintol contacts Anibuna's second-in-command. Australia is emptied of Limies. Using the Games animal handlers, the Limies are scattered all over the planet in close proximity to every Poltox Base. The Limies are unconscious when they are dumped in groups of fifty to a hundred near each brood group's dome.

On awakening, the little monsters smell the Poltox and go nuts. They know through some kind of previously ingrained instinct that the green fence is deadly, so they find a suitable area nearby the domes and start digging their burrows. Already pups are being born. These little imps can fend for themselves from day one and munch away at worms and insects inside the burrows. Scouts keep watch on the Poltox day and night. Foraging parties scour the surrounding area for food tearing into the local wildlife like a bushfire. Into this new environment lands one thousand Hitori hunters. They have not been told of the extra Limies that are roaming the planet.

"Annnd there, you have it, Games fans. Day one of Anibuna Nineties' week-long hunting safari is about to begin. The Hitori hunters have all been allocated a preserve. The betting is open. Let the hunt commence." Sparyten's beak-splitting grin flashes on the screen.

From the Azores staging area, the thousand Hitori and their twelve allotted Thibrans streak off to their individual hunting grounds eager to get to grips with the game allocated to their individual preferences. Almon and his three, class four hunting buddies are after Limies and land in sector seven to begin their hunt. They all have rapid-firing point-one scatter guns. These eight-barrel weapons are specially designed for hunting Limies. They put out a phenomenal number of pulses. The pulses are only point-one, but that is more than enough to kill a small Limie. As backup weapons, they carry point-four pistols.

Each of the four hunters carries a pheromone sensor which picks up the unique scent given off from the Limies. They smell like battery acid. A very stringent smell. Although if you can smell it strongly, you are in deep Gromal shit. For at that point, you are probably surrounded.

Kownn's sensor picks up traces of Limie. He signals his partners over their comms units. They converge on his position and fan out. The signal leads them to a single-storey white-painted building with weird two-wheeled contraptions sitting outside of it. There are some bones scattered around one of the things with a cage attached to it. The meter picks up a strong reading from the cage and bones. The hunters look at each other and tighten their grips on the RFLGs (rapid-firing Limie guns). Three cover the fourth who keeps his eyes on the meter. Their forty-eight Thibrans are in a clump behind them. They have grav-plate carriers which are loaded with all of their gear, plus they are all armed with point-one pistols as backup defence.

Kownn waves the handheld scanner in front of him. There is a strong reading from inside the building. He orders six of his Thibrans to go in and check the dwelling. The cheery Thibrans run in to carry out their master's wishes, totally oblivious to the danger associated with the Limies. A few minutes later, one pops his head out and cheerily shouts, "It is all clear."

# Kentucky National Guard Building, Harlan County

Brood group one-eight-nine landed beside the disused National Guard Building just south of Harlan on Highway 421. The big craft settled neatly in the open space behind the building complex. The energy fence deployed encloses the troop ship and the building which they cleared and are now using as their barracks.

The security gate of the energy fence faces Professional Lane, which runs the length of the building's flank. Brood Trooper Finter is on his second hour of his six-hour guard stint and is already bored to tears wishing something would happen to relieve the monotony. During times like this, he would think fondly of his hatchling hood friend Shoull. He often wondered what had become of him.

A pair of Limies latch onto his leg dragging him from his daydream. This is not what he had meant, by wishing something would happen. Grabbing the little reptiles, he tears them off his leg with a grunt of pain and smashes them together killing them both. He hits the button to close the fence just as he is starting to pass out from blood loss. His last memory is calling out for his brood leader's help.

"He is starting to come around, brood leader Anizod," states Milor, the medic.

"Uh-Huh."

"The bites to the inside of his legs severed arteries. We have a lucky trooper here, sir."

"Uh-huh."

"He will require some extended time in a surgical unit before he is fit for duty. I will go and make sure he is okay."

"Uh-Huh."

The medic trots back to his bay in the heart of the ship. His fellow medic Bunni asks him what 'Uh-Huh' said about the scale-ripping Limies. Milor laughs at the inside joke they all play with the taciturn brood leader. "He said Uh-Huh as usual." They both laugh; no one has heard their commander speak more than six words at any given time.

"Brood leader Anizod, we have just received a communication from these idiot Games people. Now, they tell us about the two hundred Limies they dropped into this area for their so-called hunters to chase down. I have told them of our injured trooper and expect compensation for his injuries. They said to take that up with Anibuna."

"Uh-Huh."

The Games channel cuts from its regular programme. Sparyten's well-known face fills the screen. In a serious voice, he starts his spiel.

"Annnd, there you have it. Games fans. We have just received word from the Gishma that the blockade of Thera Three is to be re-established and the hunt is to be cut short. We have not been notified of further hunts or why the hunt has been shortened. A portion of the ticket price will be refunded, and the wagers already paid will be returned to individual accounts through the MTS; stay tuned for more as it happens, Games fans."

# Anibuna's Conquest Ship The Anun

The 'Anun' is a massive craft. Much bigger than a battleship. It boasts a hanger deck holding eighty, multi-environment FD 40 fighter bombers. Six heavily armoured troop transporters and six talons, consisting of four hundred and eighty Anunnaki Marines. The name said it all. This is a conquest vessel, and it is ideally suited to that task.

While Anibuna is in overall command, he is more of an administrator. It's Captain Wolknun who runs the military side of the ship, and he is exceptionally good at it.

The gentle-voiced Wolknun gives his first order. "Crew! Set the ship to battle stations."

Green lights flash throughout the great ship as the crew race to their battle stations. Heavy blast doors close off vital sections of the vessel. Within minutes, the well-trained crew have the ship ready for combat.

In the Command Control Room, Wolknun sits in his motorised command chair which is on a raised lozenge-shaped platform that goes from one side of the room to the next. The chair is on rails and can slide from end to end enabling him to move along its length to better see his operator's stations below his level, situated at the flat end of the 'D' shaped room. Behind him are two heavy durasteel blast doors. Two armed Marines stand guard at each side of the sliding doors. In front of him is an identical but lower lozenge-shaped platform containing his two helm officers.

Around the curving wall of the 'D' are his weapons, comms, and shield stations. All the operators are professionals and keen to show their well-liked, gentle-voiced captain what they can do.

A massive, curved screen shows a tactical display of the area around the ship. Thera Three's blue and white globe is bang in the middle. A small green glowing spaceship on the display shows the position of the Belatan battleship. Scans show it is unshielded and is powered down to just station-keeping energy levels. It is sitting in the same orbit as the Anun, on the exact opposite side of the planet.

"Weapons! Arm two Clawswipe Sixties," orders Wolknun calmly.

"Weapons Aye! Two Clawswipe Sixties armed and awaiting guidance."

"Target coordinates. Have each missile go out along this orbital plain from each direction, so we hit the Belatan ship simultaneously from each side." Wolknun leans forward in his chair as he issues the order.

"Weapons aye, same orbital, but opposite paths, simultaneous launches to bisect the target at the same time."

"Wait for my command. Comms, get me the Belatan Captain. Weapons, fire on my hand signal. I will be distracting their captain and their comms operator at the same time. We don't want them sending a distress call. Watch for my raised claw. Weapons."

"Weapons aye, awaiting signal."

"Comms aye, sending now."

Wolknun slides his chair along the lozenge-shaped platform until he is over his comms officer's station.

On the Belatan Peacekeeping Ship, Captain Vertenex is called to the comms station. On the screen is a purple-feathered Anunnaki

"Belatan Captain. We need to talk about this situation with the release of Limies down on Thera Three." Wolknun raises his clenched fist, giving the launch signal.

Two ultra-fast missiles streak away from the Anun's weapons bay, going in different directions around the planet. Wolknun is still talking away to Captain Vertenex when the speaker gives out a shriek of static.

"Status," snaps Wolknun.

"Target destroyed, sir."

"Comms," Wolknun says in a gentler voice.

"Comms aye, no messages sent from the target vessel, sir."

"Excellent, well done, everyone. Stand down from battle stations. Launch the suppression web satellites and initiate the pulses when I give the command. Comms, contact the Boldonian, Stex Va-D and inform him his enterprise will not be impaired. Tell the Games people to finish up today because we are going to re-establish the blockade awaiting the arrival of Lord Feydon's Occupation Force Fleet."

A chorus of aye aye's comes over the speakers in the Command Control Room. Wolknun sits back in his chair, his tail contently twitching. A particularly good start, and all collected on his ship's internal brag-bag. He holds the forty-two slot in the Gishma Naval Rankings. This could see him elevated. You never know.

Down on Thera Three, the midnight sky over the Pacific Ocean lights up with the bloom of a mini super-nova. No Andrend Poltox or anyone else really, saw the big Belatan ship do a surprisingly good if short-lived imitation of the Sun. Eight hours later, Dangon the Maxus brood group ground commander is informed of a missed communications slot by the battleship. Comms gear is checked for malfunctions. There are none. The ship in low orbit can be seen from the ground. It's gone. An emergency meeting is held by the senior brood leaders to determine what may have happened. Midway through the meeting, all of the power goes off.

# Mars Orbit

Atinus calls Zin for an update. She is in Mars orbit and wants to know the way things are back on the moon before she brings her ship in. Zin tells her of the large explosion that their sensors picked up. They are going to check it out with the SRC51 and then get back to her.

The SRC51 stealth craft lands back in the hangar after doing a drive-by to see what had happened. They had picked up the massive explosion on sensors, but have no idea of what it may have been. The debris field showing where the Belatan battleship used to be answers that question, but not what caused it.

"Zin, the Belatan blockade ship. It's gone! There's nothing here but radioactive dust."

"What about the scale ticking Anunnaki, Brakk?"

"We will do a full orbit and see what's there."

"Be careful."

"We will, Zin."

The clever little shielded craft does a full orbit and notices some weird things. The Anunnaki are laying out the suppression satellites again. In the same low orbit as before. What's surprising is the lack of response from the large heavily armed Boldonian Orbital Warehouse that is sitting in a higher orbit in full sight of the shuttles laying the suppression web. The only reasonable explanation is that the Boldonians are in on whatever is happening. They return to Eden Base passing the large Anunnaki vessel which is now in geo-sync orbit above the Azores sSpaceport.

# Harlan County

Four Hitori are tracking the Limies. Their RFLGs are tearing up the little groups as they come upon them. They have worked their way down Highway 119, then turned right and started to follow the little reptiles down the four-twenty-one. Between them, they have bagged seventy-two Limies. They decide to stop for a break where a river runs close to the road they have been walking down. They turn off the highway and walk down Industrial Park Road. Their Thibrans quickly set up camp. The hunters go down to examine the river. It's a novel experience for them as the Hitori home world is one of the most arid of all of the Anunnaki worlds. All of them are playing like hatchlings in the shallow clean running water. Then all of a sudden everything turns to Gromal shit.

Two hundred odd miles above them a technician on Wolknun's ship presses a button which activates the suppression web.

The Thibrans start shouting in alarm as the four grav-plates suddenly drop to the ground with a heavy thump barely missing crushing the Thibrans that were guiding them. Nothing is working. No lights, no pheromone sensors, no radio, no cooking facilities by way of their portable replicator, no refrigerator for keeping their purple beer cold and no hard-light weaponry for keeping them safe from the ravenous little Limies. Then as if planned to coincide with the loss of all the electronics, the four comrades detect a strong battery acid smell, and little chirping noises can be heard all around them. Seconds later, the screaming starts.

Four miles down the same road, the Andrend mercenary's energy fence blinks out. Inside the troop transporter, everything goes dark. Then flickering green emergency lights come on illuminating some very concerned Poltox.

Trooper Runilon just started his guard rotation when the energy fence's protective green shimmer just flicked out completely. He immediately calls into his wrist communicator for the brood leader to come to the airlock when he notices the power indicator on the comms unit is blank. He quickly and professionally checks his weapon; it too is totally dead. With the lightning-fast reactions engineered into the Andrend, he rips the rifle off its sling and bats a rushing Limie away from his body, but there are too many following it. He screams back into the ship for help. His cry of alarm from the gate turns into screams of pain as he is overwhelmed and ripped to pieces by the fast little carnivores.

With no working weapons, the pulse rifles just become awkward clubs. Six of the Andrend troopers are lost before the airlock can be manually closed, and even then, five little ones get through the gap. These are killed inside the ship. It's noted with worry that they are very young which means the bangerups are already producing offspring at their normal prodigious rate. All Poltox know how fast these things breed and the dangers they pose from memories and stories from their own history.

Sparyten and his production crew from the games broadcasting channel are on their way to the spaceport in a transport skimmer when it suddenly falls out of the sky. Luckily enough, they are only fifty feet off the ground and apart from some bumps and bruises, everyone is okay which is good from the Limies' point of view, because they like to tenderise their own meat.

The Limies pour into the downed craft tearing into the occupants as they are trying to recover from the shock of the impact that tore open the burrow the Limies constructed near the Poltox security dome in the spaceport. Very young Limies can only take little nibbles. Their parents leave plenty of flesh on the bones for them to do so. Sparyten has delivered his last broadcast. His beak is wide open in his trademark cute grin. The little Limie peeking out of it just adds to the cuteness.

# Dovernn One
# Gishma Clan Leader

Dovernn calls a meeting of all the Anunnaki on Thera Three to lay out his strategy for stripping the planet and holding it against any Alliance interference.

"Gishma!" cries Dovernn One. Staring with his fierce eyes into the view screen camera's pick-up. "We are going to step up our plundering of this resource, so no more side-tracking with hunts or games. We are here for the plunder, Anibuna. Lay off the alcohol. Coordinate the mining. Joadin, you and Doplon get as many Adamex working as possible. Send down the backup units you have in storage on Eden. The Limies will take care of the Poltox scum and any loose Adamu that are still unaccounted for. Joadin, terminate the Adamu you brought up to Eden Base. They are no longer of any concern. Your experiments are no longer necessary."

"Anibuna, set up energy fences around our mine sites and the Adamex breeding areas to keep the Limies from interfering with production. Feydon's blockade fleet is being assembled and will leave soon. Wolknun's conquest class ship should be more than enough to hold the planet until help arrives. The Boldonians have been bought by giving them a safe transit channel through the suppression web to their orbital warehouse, plus they will supply the entire fleet with all the supplies we will need over the predicted two hundred years or so that this venture will last for. That should keep the storekeepers off our backs."

He takes a deep breath and continues in a more serious tone, "Those are your orders. See that you carry them out. Advancements in rank are guaranteed if successful. Do not let me down." Then with a final steely-eyed stare into the camera, the head of the Gishma clan screams, "GISHMA!"

# Eden Base

Zin sits watching Dovernn One's speech. "Well, we now know what the scale-ripping bangerups are up to. We are cut off again due to the suppression web. At least we know our cover here is intact, and the data got back to Randor with the two SID tail lifters. The Anunnaki think Eden Base is still under their control."

"True, but what do we do now?"

"We stop the bangerups, Cydon. That's what we do."

A great cheer rises from all the friends and comrades in the large conference room.

"Death to the Anunnaki."

### The End